Also by Paula Tully

Meeting Countess Markievicz and Other Irish Short Stories

HER REBEL SELF

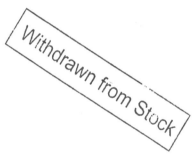

Paula Tully

Her Rebel Self

Published by Orchid Press

© Paula Tully 2018

Cover design by Kristen Lockley at
www.fossdesign.co.uk

For May and Michelle

Contents

Waiting for Fire
Monday, 1ˢᵗ November 1920

The men I know are coming for me must be dead inside. With their brutal impulse to burn and rampage their way through our rural towns and villages. The hunt has now turned to the men and boys and women of Dublin city; all of us as noble to them as pustular rats. Well, I'm ready for their drunken taunts about traitors and fugitives. Their morbid threats and imperious fire-waving. The Auxies have been drilled with a lethal refinement you might not find in the military's bawdier Black and Tans. The Tans is the name the murderous lot of them have been given by our people.

The rumour weaving itself between the safe house women is that the streets around Guinness's are not being targeted again this week. So I was willing yesterday to bribe young Mary with anything she wanted to go with my mother to Aunty Kathleen's house near the brewery for a few days. Mary said the only thing she wanted was for me to be careful, whatever my reason for needing to be alone in the house.

Today, like most in the city, the three of them are mourning the passing of the young Barry boy after his early morning hanging in Mountjoy Prison. Imagine it, the first execution by the English military since the Rising, over four years ago. The thought of Kevin Barry's young, dawn-gallowed skin growing colder by the hour makes me pull tighter the collar of my long overcoat round my own neck.

I'm still baffled by who sent me that anonymous note, telling me about this second military attack on the house. On me. The authorities must think I know every last detail of what my brothers have been doing for the cause. What with the generous help, it seems certain, of Edmund's father and his relentless digging into my life. Well, they'd be half right if the last couple of days are anything to go by. I had to leave John hiding in that freezing shack of a shed last night, the slow rasp and grip of something infected inside his blood. And I know he was about to tell me that our Seamus played a part in the ambush on those soldiers, outside the bakery, back in September. Why else has he disappeared on us, again? I've always known what my brothers are, what they've done, and I'm no different. Their absence from our lives has drained this house of its fierce hulk of boisterous demands.

My immediate dread is for young Mary who I hope is still with my mother and Kathleen outside the prison, with countless others, a show of mass solidarity and support for Kevin Barry and his family, and the other political prisoners, on such a tragic occasion. I was there myself only yesterday with the other Cumann na mBan members. We were busy getting hot dinners into some of the remand prisoners; those all but condemned men allowed the luxury of a decent food parcel. Later, we all stood there in the chilling clutch of the evening and waited; some believed a late reprieve was possible. Kevin's sister, Kathleen Barry, and her friends sang songs, knowing that Kevin and the others would be listening, would no doubt be deeply comforted by the melancholy chords stretching up from between the prison gates.

I imagine Mary absconding from my mother and strutting gaily through her own back door, into this front room, at the wrong time, the appalled look on her fourteen year old face as she witnesses the dumb barbarism of the Tans. A morose heaviness coats the cold air around me like a dreadful message waiting to be delivered. Let the blackguards come very soon then, is what I say.

The main street below the hill has emptied itself of its usual morning clamour; even the trams appear to have trundled off elsewhere. Not a sinner from any of our steep avenues with business of their own has passed up or down outside our house this last hour. If it's not Mountjoy they've taken themselves off to, it'll be one of the early All Saints' Day services. Your brave soul will find itself in good company, Kevin.

While I absorb the quiet emptiness, my fingers move across the scrubbed wooden table and find the familiar pages of my open diary - the others long destroyed - and I start to caress them softly as though they are fallen rose petals. I look down at the black leather bound diary. Details of recent entries are sparse, carefully banal, illegible in places, and peppered with the plain language of everyday tragedy in the streets of Dublin, and round the country; the cool reportage of death. Earlier this morning, I placed a single striking match beside the diary; one will be sufficient. But not quite yet, there should still be time.

The months reverse rapidly through my fingers like a silenced history unleashing itself, hungry to be read. My recent past, its vital elements, condensed into one last reading, a single, rapid ingestion of experience, perhaps no longer my own, before the curl of ravenous flame engulfs it, forever. I hope the distraction of reading and remembering will somehow sustain me in this fraught stillness. While I wait.

After the Easter Rising

A Promise, Monday, 9th April 1917

I heard the Christchurch bells ringing early this morning. I wonder if I'll hear them next year, their insistent, hopeful clang. That solemn sound makes me sad at any time, but much sadder this year. Glad, though, the thing itself is done. Something needed to happen. But the price of it will always be terrible.

This Easter Monday has been full of cold, sporadic showers of sleety, flakeless snow. After eleven o'clock mass, there was a brief gap in the weather, so I walked quickly down Ormond Quay, on to Bachelor's Walk, towards the upper end of O'Connell Street. As I turned the corner where the bridge meets the street, I saw the republican flag flying, half mast and illicit, from the one flagstaff which still remains over the GPO, the decrepit building itself still in ruins. Large crowds of people were assembling and reassembling, determined to mark the first anniversary of the Rising, despite General Mahon's orders against such gatherings.

An awful sensation of alarm went through me when, as I got closer, I saw the amount of young boys and girls who were throwing stones and breaking windows. A fresh downpour of grey sleet slid out of the sky and I just stood there picturing the dirty water puddling on the surface of the long shards of broken glass, which lay, almost invisible, all over the wet ground. I found shelter in a draper's doorway and watched tired workers saluting the unofficial flag and quickly going on about their ordinary business. The soldiers changing guard were stoned by young men with loud voices and contingency missiles which could be seen half concealed within their worn jackets. I prayed my brothers weren't among them. When the soldiers reached for their rifles, the men took off in every direction. Eventually, when my eyes had seen enough, I hurried across the main street, away from the trouble, and took a short cut by Lower Abbey Street to Dillon's to meet Nuala for tea.

We mulled over the year that had passed in this confined city and speculated about its future. Like everyone in the country, it seems, we're still waiting for news of the release of Eamon De Valera and the rest of the political prisoners, who are still incarcerated in British prisons across the water.

Nuala had a mischievous look to her as she entwined her long fingers round her hot teacup to squeeze off the cold, letting her gaze drift outside beyond the window. 'I wonder if they'll be let back in time to remember Thomas MacDonagh and Tom Clarke and Eamonn Ceannt, or any of the others who were shot by the government last year in Kilmainham,' she said. She turned her face slowly back towards the room. She had spoken in that overly dramatic *I-don't-care-who-hears-me* voice of hers. She'd have loved if a soldier just happened to be sitting at a table beside us. She'd have pivoted herself towards him and flashed her green eyes up and down his uniform, the challenge of her words suspended between them in the steamed air. As we sat there drinking our tea, the drawn faces of the young men who were actually sitting next to us hinted they might've been wondering the same thing about Dev and the others.

All this talk of prisoners and prisons made me think out loud and before I knew it I was telling Nuala about my grand plan to get away from Ireland for a bit. How I was going to travel on the mail boat from Kingstown and escape to London to try something different. No more smothered guilt between my big brother and me about what he should have done, what he could have done, to save my Rory from the snipers at Jacob's, last year. A break away from John's insistence that I should only concern myself with the household. It'd be a chance, I told her, to get more experience while I figured out what I actually wanted for myself.

Nuala just stared at me as if I'd sprouted another head right there in the chair. When she opened her mouth to speak, her rapid words clamped fiercely into the subdued calm of the tearooms. 'How could you even allow such unpatriotic thoughts to enter your mind, girl? Doesn't your family and country need you, now, more than ever, what with so many of our men gone? Running away to England from your own private troubles isn't the answer, Dervla Kelly. Imagine having such unnatural ideas, and from a girl who spends so much of her spare time with her head stuck in the *Freeman's Journal*, and more beyond.'

I suppose Nuala was right to say those things, one or two of them I'd rather not dwell on, to be brutally honest. I did try to lighten the mood a bit. 'Ah now, Nuala, don't be upset with me, I'm only imagining a different sort of life. Sure couldn't I get secret work from the Gaelic League and bring down the entire British ruling class from a tiny scullery in Mayfair?' I touched her forearm lightly and tried to catch her eye. She didn't find any of it amusing. She seemed more interested in looking at her reflection in the butter knife so she could pin back long strands of that curly red hair of hers which had come loose during her little outburst. But I knew she wasn't finished with me yet.

'Dervla, you're talking about venturing yourself over to London, the imperial city of our oppressive enslavers. You tell me this: what are they doing here, in Ireland? They have no need to be here, to occupy our nation, to drench us in their laws and culture. You know all this and yet still you talk of our enemy's lair as being some kind of playground for your personal notions.'

This is the Nuala I will miss if I do go. The burn and truth of her passion is boundless. But it's *her* passion. I think I need to suspend mine for a while, until I'm more ready. We will always share the same republican goals, more so now that Home Rule has been pushed away from us again. So I promised her today in the tearooms that if I do leave, I will be back in time to stand with her, to do what we can to continue the job of taking back what is rightfully ours. I told her this time we'd stand tall beside the men, not crease their shadows in the background of the next uprising. Well, at least that last bit made her smile.

Now that I'm finally back in the house, I feel I've let an important day go by without doing enough, and I'm feeling guilty and tired of it all. Should I have dragged Nuala out onto O'Connell Street to pick up stones with the others? To prove to her I meant what I said about coming home. Now, I find myself imagining that other life, a brighter, more vibrant one, in London. Free from all this melancholy and dreadful loss. The constant mourning of our lack of freedom is a hard thing to take, day in day out. Even with the growing support for the imprisoned Volunteers. And, anyway, Lord knows, I could do with earning more money. They say there is no end to the amount of jobs in London, what with the European war taking most of the men out of England.

Release, Monday, 18th June 1917

In the predawn hours of yesterday morning, I was woken up by the raucous noise of crowds thumping forward along the footpaths and narrow roads outside my bedroom window. It just didn't occur to me at the time, which was no human time at all, what on earth was going on. I heard an urgent push of anticipation in clumps of passing voices, an expectant rumble of something new in the air; a kind of elation. Then it hit me. The rest

9

of the Easter Rising prisoners have been released; they're finally on their way home to us from the English prisons. Those people rushing by outside the house and down the hill towards the main street were going to meet them arriving in at the North Wall.

I jumped out of bed, got dressed in a violent hurry, and followed the stragglers outside on the road. When we arrived at the quayside, there was a torrent of confusion flying around as to which port this last group of prisoners was arriving in at. In the end, we traipsed on further to Westland Row to meet the mail train from Kingstown. Such crowds spilling onto the road and paths when we eventually got there.

We waited for nearly three hours very close to the entrance. The prisoners finally arrived at 9am into the railway station. Some I didn't know at first - the loss of beards and their shaved heads made a great change in their appearance - as they were shepherded out of the station. Tom Kelly and Winny O'Connell were just the same. De Valera was just the same. One frail looking man had to be carried off the train and through the station. I saw one young lad standing alone in the midst of the commotion simply break down and cry like a lost child. I felt so sorry for each of them. Some were genuinely stunned by the ecstatic crowds; their freedom was made real.

How my heart broke for Mrs Connolly and Mrs Pearse and Mrs Clarke when I saw them clinging to each other, crying, unable to hide their bitter grief. It must have been so very hard for them with no-one coming home into their outstretched arms; not like these rebels, or the ones lucky enough to have survived the Rising, as John and Seamus had.

As I stood in the noisy crush of so many people, I thought about the terror of death, what those brave men must have endured in their final moments in the stone breakers' yard, the shouted order for the firing squad to take aim. And so many ordinary people whose startled flesh was ruptured by stray bullets. There was nothing ordinary about my Rory, of course. He'd wanted the Rising to make a man of him. But that sniper's bullet outside Jacob's interrupted his grand plans.

I didn't go to work yesterday, I felt I could not. My elation had turned to depression at the memory of my beloved Rory, his Volunteer friends, and the civilians who are gone.

Dublin's Countess, Thursday, 21st June 1917

After work today, still with an immense relief in my heart for the released prisoners, I joined an enormous mass of people at Westland Row to see Countess Markievicz coming home. Finally, she has been released from Aylesbury Prison in England. Such crowds. Such cheering. It looked like thousands of workers made their way to the station to welcome her back to Ireland.

As I moved slowly through the heaving body of people, I caught snippets of stories about Madame's generosity and hard work during the dreadful days of the employer Lockout, a few

11

years ago. Familiar tales of her collecting money for the starving families who had lost almost everything. I know some don't like her eccentric ways, but I've always admired the woman.

I remember a year or so after the Lockout, when we used to watch the formidable Countess marching through the streets with her Fianna boys, or with the Citizen Army, wearing her dark green uniform and her hat pinned on one side with the little insignia of the workers' union, the red hand. I wonder did she ever imagine then that she'd be fighting the military like a man on the same streets a couple of years later.

She's been described as an inspiration to people all over Ireland. Her call to women, years before the Rising, to take their active place in the struggle for this nation, to seek out their niche which is waiting for them in the building of a free Ireland. But even with this summer's prison releases, it feels to me like those niches have been crudely filled in with more English cement, this past year.

But I'm not going to let these sombre notions overshadow an important celebration. You couldn't see the ground beneath your feet today; it felt like the whole country had descended upon Dublin. The noise was like the booming sound of human happiness; a new sound to savour after so much despair. It's a real pity I didn't get close enough to meet Countess Markievicz earlier, to shake her hand and wish her well.

Afterwards, I went to Nuala's for supper. She'd invited me as we hadn't seen each other for weeks. Her mother handed me a steaming plate of succulent lamb chops served with boiled buttered potatoes. I could feel the two of them waiting for me to say something; they obviously saw the surprise in my eyes. Nuala winked at me and said the food was a special celebration for all the releases this year. While we ate, she pressed me for every detail of today's great homecoming.

I got home late. I have to say, a fierce excitement runs through the city as I write this entry. But how long it will last is anybody's guess.

An order from Dublin Castle, Sunday, 29th July 1917

For the last two weeks I've been so busy helping my mother with the housekeeping, as well as doing extra sewing alterations at work, and for Central Branch. Some evenings have been very late. The tiredness got the better of me the other night when I burned a Cumann na mBan uniform skirt I'd been working on. The trouble of it made me want to cry like a chastised toddler and rip it up and remake the whole skirt from scratch. But it didn't come to that. That night I got home after 12.30. It was too late for the tram. To think that my own mother had been out walking the streets looking for me. I felt terrible about this as it was a very wet night. Her vigilance - usually reserved for John and Seamus - stopped her from sleeping well that night.

The household income is another constant worry for my mother. The price of eatables is shocking these days. Everyone says far too much of the good stuff goes off to England at the North Wall. Enough cash is sometimes hard to come by so I have to take whatever extra alterations work I can when it's offered.

I'm still waiting for a letter from that Waterford housekeeper who advertised on behalf of an English family for a live-in job near London; it's been weeks since I applied for it. If they offer it to me, I'll take it for a few months and save some decent money to bring back with me.

The desire to get away from this drudgery gets stronger each week. I need to do something different for myself. I'm proud of what my brothers did for Ireland last year, of course I am, for heaven's sake, but what about me? Do I have to remain chained to the same life, forever? As it is, John still isn't keen on me going with the other girls to the C na mB meetings and drill practice. He says no good can come of my membership because some of *those women* are becoming too militant. Too militant! I bet he wouldn't dare refuse our involvement with the Sinn Féin clubs, though: tireless fundraising activities, catering for the concerts, mending the IV uniforms. None of it paid work. Sinn Féin is different when it comes to women, he says. Meaning of course that, along with all the support, they're also happy to let us do the boring menial work. Even so, does he not want me to do what I can for the Volunteers? While I'm still here, that is.

At least Seamus takes more of an interest in what I do. If I do go to England, I'll really miss our chats about our beloved country, what it means to be tied to another with all its broken promises of Home Rule. And about the pure idea of total independence. He told me he understood the literature I sometimes gave him much better when we talked it over together, that I made our turbulent history more meaningful to him.

Early yesterday evening, I went up to the Phoenix Park for a walk. A couple of wild deer watched from the trees, alert for a tiny shift in the warm air. Near the Wellington Monument, there was guarded talk among some young men. Andy Moore was among them, so I went over to say hello. Andy looked tired and distracted. He told me the Dublin Metropolitan Police had been lining up to stop an Irish Volunteer procession coming from the Dublin Mountains earlier in the day. But the police were unexpectedly dismissed by Dublin Castle before any of our boys passed by. That didn't make much sense to me at all. Andy and the young men had also heard that the government had issued another order from the Castle: no hurleys to be carried, or kilts, or uniforms to be worn by Irish Volunteers during route marching. Could it be that the Castle decided to let the Volunteers have their last ceremonial outing? The boys won't take well to this new scratching away of their national pride.

I took my time walking home. I wanted to measure the weight of what I'd heard at the monument with my own thoughts. There's been a furtive shift in the mood and patience of this city, recently. A kind of galvanizing of things, not only since the release of the prisoners, but also since poor Mrs McDonagh's funeral mass earlier this month in the Pro Cathedral.

There were great crowds there for her, not that she'd ever know it now, God love her. The Irish Volunteers had formed a guard of honour in the church. I'm sure she would marvel at such a spectacle laid on for her while the lime-charred remains of her rebel son lay in a godless grave. Her body had been brought by train the same day as I refereed a camogie match in Croke Park. She will never see her grandchildren play a national sport, nor indeed fight for their country's freedom, as her son did last year.

The days before the funeral had also been tense with anticipation about the East Clare election results. De Valera, now a free man, came in on top, as expected, thank God. C na mB gave great support in the elections work. I wonder what it is, though, that my senses are telling me tonight about my dear old city. If Dublin is shifting towards something new, how deep and jagged will the fissures be this time? For God's sake, we are still recovering from the bloodshed and total destruction of last year.

The Last Dance, Friday, 17th August 1917

At last night's céilí in no. 41, Nuala and I spent most of the time dancing together, and talking. We ignored the intermittent advances of the young Volunteers. Some of them had a bit of drink taken but they behaved themselves well enough. They had been doing their drill practice earlier in the evening. An array of hurleys stood quietly to attention against the back wall.

The third and fourth Battalions take their drilling very seriously. Seamus is always talking about the pure excitement brimming in the boys' eyes now that all the prisoners are free. The drill halls round the city are filling up every week with new Volunteers, he's been saying. It felt like most of them were at the céilí in the York Street hall last night. Clumps of young men sitting and talking and smoking, no doubt planning the next few parades, now that the Dublin Brigade is reorganizing. The whole of the city it seems is looking to a future where they might dare to see the back of the British administration.

When I told Nuala what Andy said a few weeks ago at the monument about the Castle's new order for no uniforms or hurleys or kilts during Volunteer marching, she said she wasn't a bit surprised. 'They'll try to suffocate us out of existence with their new orders for no this and no that. Fools they are if they think they can stop the force of the regroupings, the new members, the new support from young and old. All we need to do is adapt ourselves to the changing conditions of the enemy. To be ready for a new uprising. A bigger one.' She spoke with such fervour and eloquence. I envy her single-mindedness, her absolute commitment to a cause I suppose I've been trying to renavigate my way through this past year. I wasn't about to dampen her spirits with odd little selfish doubts about my own course in this new marshalling of the movement.

Last night's céilí was all about me and Nuala having a bit of fun. And we did. We jumped in and out of the dancing, swapping back and forth so that we'd mostly end up as partners. The accordion players upped the tempo skilfully so that by the time everyone had joined the lines, the entire hall vibrated to the fierce stomp and rhythm of the music. Our music. I felt great waves of nostalgia for our childhood, for our teenage years, as we linked arms and laughed and twirled round the other couples.

When we sat back down for the last time, I knew the hour had come to tell Nuala my move to London was now definite. One way or another, I was going very soon and my decision was made. She was good enough not to blanket me with a lecture about duty and republicanism, not to flail and rant about our ravaged nation, our subjugated people. Thank God for sparing me all that. But the expression in her beautiful eyes told me she already knew I understood these things. 'Just come back for when we really need you. Because we *will* need you, Dervla,' was the only thing she said.

Let me Go, Saturday, 15th September 1917

I told Mam and the lads about my plan to move to London next month. That was a few hours ago and they haven't said that much to me in the meantime. Of course, John and Seamus already knew I had applied for a job and that I was looking in the newspapers for other positions.

They just sat quietly at the table and listened to me going on about the money I'd be able to send home from my new job. I obviously wouldn't be doing any war work for the British, it was a normal job in service in one of those big houses outside London, and there may even be some seamstress work available. I told them not to give it a second thought, that I'd be back home in no time at all.

I even joked that when I got back I'd marry a nice Irish man and settle down in my own house. Mam looked at me and smiled when I said that. The image, no doubt, of me with a family of my own flashed across her mind. Grandchildren with a better future than her own children. At the same time she glanced over at Mary who was sitting close to John. Did she half expect her youngest to eventually go across the same water as her sister? To wait a few short years and then be sitting with the rest of her family, like today, announcing her own imminent departure?

While I was talking, Mam stood up and busied herself by undoing her apron, straightening it back into its fold at the waist and retying it neatly at the back, as she often does when she's listening to one of us. She came towards me and put her hand on my shoulder. 'I know things are hard and there's not much money to go round, so if you want to make a go of it in England, Dervla, I won't stand in your way.' That was the only encouragement I needed. I stood up and hugged her and silently thanked her for being so brave. Because I know it wasn't easy for her to let me go like that. But then again, maybe, in some strange way, she thought I'd be safer in England with there being so much unrest here in Ireland against the Castle authorities.

John wasn't as supportive, though. He was like a male incarnation of Nuala when I first mentioned the idea to her. 'How could you consider moving to a city which is a constant target for German air raids, not to mention the hardships ordinary people suffer through endless hours of work and food shortages?' He spoke of me placing myself in a foreign danger he couldn't protect me from. There it is, Rory's ghost, once again, haunting him about that night.

But I could have killed John with the steel glare in my eyes; he should have had a bit more tact in front of Mam and Mary. I calmly told him that the job was a good distance away from the actual city and that I'd have some free time and that of course I'd manage. Aren't we all suffering enough hardship here in our own city? A regular income would really help. He broke my stare by turning to Mary to ask what she thought of her big sister leaving the nest.

'Well, I'm delighted for her! She'll have a bit of an adventure in the big city,' she said to our older brother. 'Just let her go, sure you can't stop her.' My little sister, bless her, had looked right at me while saying all this. At least John had the decency not to destroy her happy optimism, a precious thing this house needs during these strange, uncertain days.

What I didn't tell John was that maybe it was

time for us to have a break from each other. I didn't tell him that, yes, there are moments, like today, that I do feel anger and frustration about the circumstances of Rory's death that night at the factory. I didn't tell him that in the darkest crevices of my subconscious mind there is a tiny gnawing spot where I blame him for that bullet.

As First Lieutenant, why didn't he question McDonagh's command to send my Rory, alone, out of the towering cover of the biscuit factory garrison, onto the too quiet street, convinced that the deliberately dropped biscuit tins from the high windows, moments before, would have instantly triggered shots from any waiting snipers? Why didn't he offer to accompany Rory to the garrison outposts to report back *together* on any signs of enemy approach round Camden Street and Patrick Street, two of the main routes into the city from Portobello and Wellington Barracks?

Nor did I tell him that the bare facts of Rory's death slice painfully within me every time I think of that last order he followed.

So perhaps it's best if I'm not around for a while, at least not until I am ready to seal off that crevice in my torn mind and listen to what my real-life consciousness tells me about my treasured older brother, a quiet patriot who also lost one of his closest friends that night.

'I suppose you feel the same, Seamus?' said John.

'Sure Dervla is already twenty four, she may never get this chance again. And the sooner she goes, the sooner she'll be back. And you know

yourself, John, our own wages don't go very far.'
He looked at John for a long moment and then
opened his mouth as if to say something more,
but changed his mind and looked away. Anyway,
after hearing what Mam and Seamus and Mary
said earlier today, I felt a warm surge of protective
love towards them. They stood up for me. And I
know John will eventually be okay with me
leaving. Even he - a young Volunteer who fought
the military last year - knows he can't keep me
totally safe and secure from the world for much
longer.

End of One War

In Service, Saturday, 24th November 1917

Well, today marks the end of my sixth week in
England. The physical act of leaving Ireland made
a small, weeping lesion in my soul. It felt as
though I was shedding my warm, familiar skin and
leaving it crumpled and torn in the rubble of my
heartbroken city. All I could do was watch from
the mail steamer the festering wound that was my
Dublin. An abandoned city raw and infected with
fractured idealism after the rebellion. In front of
my eyes, its contours disappeared slowly as the
heaving tide pulled me towards the steel-grey
horizon. For the first three weeks or so I
wondered if I'd made an awful mistake.

I've been working all the hours God sends, as a
housemaid, in a tightly-run house on Burdelton
Road, miles beyond London's eastern parameters.
There is so much dirt and dust in the heavy
carpets and some days all I seem to be doing is
boiling endless pots of water for one thing or
another. There hasn't been a lot to write about at
all. I suppose my room is okay, at least it's
relatively warm, situated up here, below the attic,
on the third floor, away from the clamour and
rush of the rest of the house. Not that it matters,
nobody really talks to me that much, anyway.

At first, I was glad of it - just keeping myself to
myself - but now I'm not so sure if I want that
kind of loneliness. Or even if I can do anything
about it. It's as if, to my employers, I'm just

another service girl from Ireland, one that's probably a bit older than expected, not really worth getting to know as a real person. Even the English housekeeper looks down her long nose at me. She doesn't include me in any of the kitchen gossip and now she's started to make fun of my accent in front of the others. She makes out she's joking, stroking my arm as though I am an obedient house pet, but I don't see the funny side of it. Only the other morning, when she made her horrible comments about my pronunciation, I literally felt my face flush red, the colour stinging itself from my neck upwards; hot tears punching from behind my eyelids. Ignorant bigot of a woman, God forgive me for saying.

So I suppose I've been finding it's easier to just keep my head down and get on with my mundane duties.

I can hear Nuala's voice shouting inside my head to stop whingeing and book my passage on the next mail boat back to Dublin. *I told you so, Dervla*, she's saying now with her head cocked to one all-knowing side, lips pursed before the next scalding: *It's bad enough at home with the social slicing of 'us' and 'them'. There's plenty of that, and more, left over from the spitting and tutting after the Rising. But you insisted on plonking yourself right in the middle of something similar, only it's much worse because it's on actual English soil.* How I miss that sweet, ranting voice.

As there's no tram line or railway station nearby, I decided a couple of weeks ago that it was time I learned how to drive a pony and car the first chance I got. Mass seemed as good a destination as any, but when I finally arrived at the church that day the service was over. A heavy shower of snow had started on the way back which made everything worse. I wished I hadn't gone. Even though the pony I borrowed was well behaved, my arms and shoulders ached for days, afterwards. But despite the worsening weather, I was determined to make a second attempt.

So, finally, last Sunday, I got there for the ten o'clock mass. It was a nice service and I got a good look at the parishioners, if that's what you'd call Catholics over here; I even said hello to some of them as we left the church. But on the way home the roads were covered in more snow than earlier that morning. The pony seemed well used to it but I suffered very much with my hands because I had to grip the slippery, semi-frozen reins with all my strength. The bitter cold pressed into every fold of skin and bone, right through my light gloves. I thought I'd cry out with the pain. When I eventually made it home, instead of a kind word from the mistress, or an offer of something hot to drink from the housekeeper, the same dull monotony of cleaning, fetching, and generally being ignored, faced me, as it has done each and every day since my arrival.

I miss Rory even more intensely these days than I did before I left. It's like I'm standing alone on a large crumbling rock in the centre of my new life, where every road and building and person rotates coolly around me. I catch myself searching for Rory's smile in other faces, or a sign of his spirit dancing in the eyes of another. But what I find is a void filled with foreign, ambivalent faces.

At least it's some consolation that perhaps this horrific war might end soon what with the British success at Cambrai. I read in yesterday's newspaper that, to celebrate the battle, the bells in St Paul's Cathedral rang out joyfully for the first time since the start of the war. More than three years of brutal European conflict is beyond comprehension.

But while I'm here I must persevere with things, I just have to, because of the money I'm able to send home every week. I'll write more when I feel up to it.

A Different Class, Tuesday, 1st January 1918

First day of the new year today.

After breakfast I put on extra layers and went to seven o'clock mass in the pony and car. Each of the men I met on the way smiled warmly and wished me heartfelt good luck for the coming year. I thought it strange as people here never usually speak to each other on the roads, not like they do at home, anyway. Usually, they're in too much of a hurry, the rhythmic clop-clop of their ponies setting the tone for the business of the day ahead. But for today the occasion was grandly marked; a fresh, talismanic bolt of good cheer for what might be a peaceful new year.

My New Year's resolution is to leave this dull job and move closer to London. I hope to get a place soon. I can't stick the provincial snobbery of my employers for much longer; their complete acceptance of it, and the way some of the other servants continue to look down on me, and the young scullery maid. Their silly pecking order annoys me, no end. I just hate the harsh, social grading of their class life. How different we are; no wonder political unity is an impossibility. I've been hearing from one or two people after mass that there are plenty of jobs in the big city for seamstresses and even housekeepers with good, clean experience. Sure aren't the Irish girls known for their domestic skills and hard work? After all, my main reason for coming to England was to live in London. I do hope this class business doesn't matter as much in London as it does out here in the lonely sticks.

The City Calls, Tuesday, 19th February 1918

I finally wrote an honest letter to Nuala. I'd been putting it off for weeks and there are only so many bland, let's-pretend-it's-all-rosy letters that can be written. I let her have a litany of my unfortunate hardships: my lonely job, the callous remarks, my homesickness, the general boredom and disappointment. She'll read my depressing letter and smile her beautiful smirk of self-righteousness as she settles down to write back telling me how things are in dear old Dublin. I actually feel much better now that I've shared my woes with Nuala.

Life's not entirely the dull catastrophe I'm making it out to be. Wasn't I lucky enough to spend my Sunday off in London? Even if it meant having to experience it on my own. I feel even more determined to move closer to the big soot-filled, noisy city I left Ireland for last year. I walked practically everywhere from Trafalgar Square to Covent Garden, back down to the Strand, along the Embankment. I looked up in awe at the Tower of London, I walked across Tower Bridge, and back again. Yes, for a few hours I felt like I was in the centre of the world, hundreds of strangers teeming and strutting around me. And, though I might have expected to, I didn't feel like a wandering lost soul.

New Friends, Saturday, 13th April 1918

My twenty fifth birthday today and would you believe it, I'm still here in England. God, I wonder where I'll be this day next year. I know I haven't written anything in ages; this diary was getting a bit too maudlin for me. But things are looking a lot better now. I finally got a position in the city and have been settling into my new life.

My digs consist of a tiny room in one of those many windowed large terraced houses in Kilburn. The new job is going as well as can be expected, I suppose; maid-of-all-work in another grand house. And I sometimes help with some of the sewing alterations. The money is better; an extra shilling an hour goes a long way. The work is often gruelling of course but I have more free time than the first job because it's not live-in. Basil Street is really close to Knightsbridge Tube station and of course the famous Harrods. Not that I'll ever set foot inside such an extravagant place, more's the pity.

My employer is a middle-aged doctor; he's good to me, I have to say. But, if I'm honest, I'm not sure about the wife yet. Something very aloof and cold about the woman. Ice-filled eyes pulled into pale brittle skin. Her amiable Irish servant girl's birthday would probably embarrass her; I can't imagine how she might react if I actually told her. No, that's not the kind of chat we'd be having. Their previous maid-of-all-work was English, and from what I can gather from the kitchen maid, she left to take up a job in one of those munitions factories - apparently the money is much better than working in service.

Lots of English women are doing men's jobs while this dreadful war still rages. We have a girl who delivers the post and the other day I couldn't believe it when I saw a whole group of women laying down tar on Oxford Street. Working with that thick, oily smell must have been nauseating for them. I can't imagine what it will be like when the men come back to England.

The second we'd finished serving the doctor and his wife their evening meal, the housekeeper said that on account of it being my birthday I could leave early. I ran out the front door and round to St Mary's and lit a candle for Ireland, and prayed that she may soon be free. It was my second such candle this week. It's become a bit of a weekly ritual for me, usually just before getting the tube at Knightsbridge to my new club.

It's called St Bride's Irish Club and they rent rooms on Fleet Street. The Wexford girl whose digs I moved into, a few weeks ago, here in Kilburn, because she was going back home, said I should become a member of St Bride's. She told me to just turn up on a Thursday evening and ask for a woman called Nellie Franny. So I did. Nellie Franny's from Kingstown and is older than me. She's tall with dark curly hair tucked into a loose bun. She has wide sensible shoulders and a gentle motherly smile. We've become good friends. There's a class in our lovely ancient Gaeilge and there are talks on most Thursdays about every aspect of Ireland imaginable. A lot like the C na mB clubs are starting to do back home. I think I'm beginning to settle into the club, it gives me something to do, and it won't harm me to make a few social connections with some of the Irish over here.

Two nights ago, the members were talking about the Bill that was passed for Compulsory Service. God in heaven, what next? The years and years of empty English promises for Home Rule and now they want to casually send our young lads off to fight and die in foreign fields of death. John and Seamus would rather lie down in the middle of the Phoenix Park and let hundreds of soldiers trample them into their own damp Irish soil.

The talk is that the Bill will be fiercely resisted in Ireland. Especially by the women in C na mB who Nellie Franny said are making a special pledge and planning parades in support of the anti-conscription campaign. She said the symbolism of hundreds of uniformed women marching through the streets will be hard for the people, and the authorities, to ignore.

In the last week or so, Nellie Franny and I have found the time to go to a few places - Kilburn Empire for the lovely old Irish ballads; the Victoria and Albert museum near Nellie Franny's work; and Buckingham Palace itself. God, I feel happier in this huge, mad city, every country you can name looking back at you in the street. I know it's all still so new to me, but already I feel younger and freer than perhaps I would be at home. Even with the constant threat of German air attacks. Is it so wrong to feel happy here in London while that horrific war on the Continent drags into its fourth year? And while my own country is still ruled by the Castle government?

The whole notion of managing without certain goods, scrimping and trying to make ends meet has been all too familiar to me and Nellie Franny, for years, so I have to say, I don't really find this new rationing too much of a hardship. And I admire some of the ordinary London women, they're resilient and hardworking, just as resourceful as any I know back home. But of course they are still very different to us. I'll write again when I get time.

Limehouse, Wednesday, 8th May 1918

Well, now I know a little of what troubles my new friend, Nellie Franny. Ever since we met in St Bride's I've felt there was a hidden sadness behind her eyes. I'm glad she opened up to me today; it's made me appreciate all the more what little time I had with Rory.

After the usual tourist stuff we'd been doing on our free afternoons, it was time to do something different.

We took ourselves off to Chinatown in Limehouse to see for ourselves what den of iniquity it truly was. The bus ride through the city to the East End wasn't long and we got there just after lunchtime.

We'd already prepared ourselves for all sorts of wickedness spilling onto the narrow streets round Pennyfields and Ming Street. The strange, narcotic waft of opium drifting from the open back doors of secret brothels and gambling parlours. Pale cockney girls with vacant expressions stepping out of alleyways and into bawdy public houses. Yellow-skinned men with long, oiled hair arguing nosily with each other in the street. Tars and deckhands from all corners of the world spitting and drinking while waiting for their merchant ships to sail them off to exotic places.

But I noticed Nellie Franny wasn't herself, she'd hardly said a word on the bus, which was unusual given our mysterious destination. After a couple of minutes of quiet walking towards the Chinese quarter, I asked her what was wrong. She saw I was determined to get an answer so she just stopped mid step and blurted out that she'd received a letter this morning from her so-called sweetheart in Belfast saying they could never be together again. Even though he was truly sorry for treating her in such a cruel way there was nothing to be done about it.

She had stopped outside a Chinese laundry shop and I couldn't help myself glancing towards the window to get a quick look at - what, exactly? I've no idea what I might have been expecting: rampant debauchery taking place between piles of rich Londoners' shirts and sheets? Thank God Nellie Franny didn't notice my lapse; she had gotten herself into a terrible state, the poor thing. She pulled the letter from her bag there and then and told me to read it for myself.

A young man called Matthew poured his heart out on the note paper. He couldn't forgive himself for leaving Nellie Franny stranded at the Kingstown mail boat all those months ago. He was utterly ashamed to tell her that his parents refused to accept a Catholic girl from the south and that he'd be instantly cut out of their will if he went ahead with his marriage plans.

I folded the letter and gave it back to her and then put my arms round her. We stood there, outside the laundry shop, and while she sobbed gently, I watched the grey London fog creep inside the dampening air.

I also noticed that a clutch of young children had gathered nearby. Radiant complexions and pitch dark eyes. Was the tall lady okay, the oldest of them enquired. I thanked her and said, yes, she'll be fine; we were just having a little chat. The children stayed where they were and remained well behaved, a sign of respect, perhaps. Nellie Franny broke our embrace to sit down on the shopfront's narrow ledge to tell me more about Matthew.

She had brought him to many of her favourite places: the pier, Killiney Hill, Dalkey village. They were madly in love and one magical summer's evening on the top of Killiney Hill, as they gazed at the huge expanse of sea, he asked her to marry him. He said they'd go to London where religion and class wouldn't matter. She couldn't wait to run away and marry him. They booked their tickets for the mail boat and she counted the days. Just before the departure date, Matthew went on one last trip by train up to Belfast to tell his family. The night before he went, he told Nellie Franny not to worry, his family would have to get over his marrying a Catholic girl. Her own parents weren't exactly overjoyed at her news, especially as they hadn't been invited to attend, but they accepted him because they had always liked him.

Their arrangement was to meet three hours before the sailing from Kingstown. Plenty of time for a pier supper. Nellie Franny sat on a wooden bench near the start of the promenade and waited for him. But Matthew didn't show up. She was utterly devastated. Where was he? She was too ashamed to go home so she just took up her luggage and stepped onto the boat, alone. In the first six months she wrote three letters to him from London, but all she received in response was silence. Until today. And what a pathetic excuse that letter contained.

Limehouse Chinatown wasn't what I'd expected. Yes, it was a bit run down here and there, but the shopfronts and footpaths were immaculate. As Nellie Franny took a second to wipe her nose with a handkerchief, I noticed a small number of oriental men going about their business. But that business seemed banal enough and not that different to how the rest of London conducted itself. Two or three of the men talked convivially among themselves outside a Chinese restaurant on the corner, behind us. I couldn't understand the elaborate Chinese lettering above the window. Others, dressed in suits and holding canes, walked in single file along the narrow street, presumably back to work, or home, after lunch. One aproned man tended to the neat display of vegetables and condiments in his grocery shop window, opposite the restaurant.

The mother of the children stepped out of a small butcher's shop next to the Chinese laundry. She was placing a package of fresh meat inside her shopping bag which itself appeared to be full of vegetables. Corralling her flock in front of her, she told them not to be bothering the nice ladies. Somewhere in her forties and still quite striking with it, if I was to guess her age. She met my eye and smiled warmly. She went to walk past us but then hesitated and asked us if it was an Irish accent she'd heard as she came out of the butcher's shop. A distinctive Dublin brogue announced itself as it brushed against the corners of her East End accent.

So we chatted to her for a few minutes. She told us she met and married a man from Shanghai nearly eighteen years ago; so many Chinese men came here to find their fortune, they still do. The youngest of their four kids is six. Not enough Chinese women in England, she said, but there are plenty of English and Irish girls who are happy to marry them instead. Getting by can be difficult at times, especially during this awful war, but they've made a happy life for themselves in Limehouse, despite the hardships. Her husband started at the docks years ago, but now he runs a respectable tobacconist shop with his brother at the far end of Ming Street.

I was glad of the distraction of the woman and her polite children - they were very interesting - because bumping into them seemed to cheer Nellie Franny up a little. She asked the woman what it was like to live in a community with so many nationalities. It seemed a bit of a personal question but the woman was keen to assure us it was - barring the odd unsavoury incident - just fine. Better than fine. Front doors are left on the latch, children play together after school, and if someone needs help they're rarely left alone. A lot like back home in Ireland, in fact. Nellie Franny sighed and told the woman and her children they were very fortunate. We declined the woman's kind offer of tea in her house as we wanted to walk round a bit more before catching our bus back to the city centre.

So, not a whiff of the satanic morals and carnal decadence described in the likes of Dickens. Our excursion to Chinese Limehouse was delightful and certainly not without its own intrigue.

I'm ending this entry thinking that Nellie Franny has had a lucky escape not being welcomed into that Ulster family.

Empire's Mothers, Friday, 24th May 1918

Today is England's Empire Day.

Hundreds of flags are strung along every building, their sharp corners snapping in the cool breeze. Empire Day - what does it even mean, any more? I wonder what the most renegade of English subjects think of their imperial history in the world of today.

Yesterday evening, in the club, the talk was of Mrs Clarke's cruel incarceration in Holloway. Another innocent victim on Dublin Castle's concocted 'German Plot' list. It would seem that the government has not tortured her poor heart enough. They now rob her of the comfort of her children, the children she worries desperately about since the shocking execution of her husband for his part in the Rising. It's some consolation, I suppose, to know that the Countess - back in prison, again - and the other women prisoners will give Mrs Clarke strength. It's a different kind of comparison, I know, and one I may not be forgiven for making, but what's happening with her makes me think of the English mothers who lost everything in another terrifying air raid four days ago in the East End.

Nellie Franny and I had arrived home from our evening walk just before the air raid started. She's been staying the odd night to have a change from her live-in room at work. Her employers don't mind as long as she's back first thing. When the dreaded siren filled the evening air everyone rushed out of their room and ran downstairs to the musty basement. The cold numbed the top half of my fingers a bluish-white but I didn't care, I knew we were safe enough.

The bombing, when it came, sounded like a thousand angry gods hurling huge, rough boulders made of solid fire towards the waiting city. It was impossible to tell where exactly the shells were landing; all we could do was listen closely for the splintering crack of falling beams and masonry and random fire bombs above our heads. None came. The air raid lasted until one o'clock in the morning. When the all-clear was given we trudged up from the dank basement and went to our rooms. But immediately after, another bomb went off. Nellie Franny said it had the sound of a final, furious shell firing itself from a disgruntled bomber. I heard later that there was a lot of damage in the East End. No mention of Limehouse but Poplar was hit badly. Lord have mercy on their souls.

I'd give anything to know what the women in Holloway make of this senseless destruction. Waiting and waiting, imprisoned in a vast, foreign city which, as things stand, imprisons their own tiny one. Empire's tight clutch and covet of its most prized colony. I'm suddenly feeling a bit tired of life. I hear the Allies are losing dreadfully. Such slaughter of men. Can such laws in our world be right? I have to say I've been thinking a lot about my family in Dublin.

Foreign Bombs, Local Bullets, Friday, 13th June 1918

I was told to leave work early today. Herself had a monstrous headache and insisted on absolute silent emptiness in the house. And because of it, to my mild astonishment, I happened to meet a handsome young Englishman.

I had decided to go to Poplar to see the awful damage for myself. I'd wanted to see the ordinary places ruined by so much bombing; the decimated site of the Upper North Street primary school, bombed exactly one year ago, and the whole street of small houses bombed just last month. I needed to see for myself what this European war looked like.

I will never forget the slow procession of pale, stunned people who were walking from Stepney and the surrounding areas in memory of those young children who perished last year. As the mourners gathered round the ruins of the school for a brief ceremony, I thought of young Mary, a good bit older, I know, but still a child like those little ones who were blown up by the Germans in their Gotha bomber. It seems too awful to comprehend such destruction of lives, and all for what? A futile earthly power that will fade, fade, fade into a dark nothingness? The whole of

London must have cried bitterly at the funerals of those little children, last year.

Later, when most of the people had left, while I was leaning against a pile of rubble which had shaped itself into a kind of stone viewing point, I saw a casually dressed, tallish looking man to my left, not much older than myself, sketching the fallen remains of what may have once been the infants' classroom, although it was impossible to tell for sure. He was half sitting on a broken wall, a drawing pad in one hand and a couple of pencils in the other. I strained to watch him work but from my vantage point I could only make out rough outlines on the pad.

I was more than slightly mortified when he suddenly stopped his work and turned his head in my direction. The late afternoon sunlight picked out chestnut strands in his straight, dark hair which parted itself naturally to one side. He stood up and smiled over at me. 'I'm just practising with the shape of the ruins and ...' He hesitated, as if he had already said too much, not used enough tact or respect. He looked up towards the vast emptiness where there should still be a roof. A solid safe cover for the lessons beneath. Not wanting to appear rude I moved closer to where he stood. 'I can't get the image out of my head, you know, of the bomb falling through the boys' classroom, then the girls' room below, before exploding just as it landed in the youngest room.' His face was still focused towards the blue summer sky. There was quiet disbelief in the sound of his barely accented words; as though he'd played the horrible scene over and over in his head, hoping it would alter, somehow.

I agreed it was such a horrific tragedy, the whole war was a terrible thing. I watched him as he carefully placed his sketch pad and pencils on the surface of a smooth rock and looked pensively into the empty spaces of dusty rubble where there should still be young, active life. He was close enough to me but seemed at a great distance in his mind. I found myself thinking I didn't want this friendly man to quickly check himself, to apologize for intruding on my afternoon, and to vanish into the city.

'You see, I haven't fought in this war. Father said I'd be more useful to the battle if I remained on home soil. But, to tell you the truth, I look at this bomb site and feel totally useless and ashamed,' he said. His shocking honesty startled me. And there was something strangely vulnerable about him. As though he'd never be able to fully burden the demands of whatever his life threw at him. I wanted to touch the skin on his arm, leave my hand there until he felt better.

Instead, I heard my voice saying, Sometimes we fight the battles we need to fight in different places, and in different ways. I was caught off guard coming out with this statement; the words just declared themselves in the warm air as if they'd been waiting to escape from a place locked within me. What had I meant by saying such a thing to this young stranger standing beside me in a part of London I'd never been to?

I made a new friend this afternoon. We sat on

a partial outer wall which had once surrounded the broken school and shared with each other many stories of our lives.

I told him of my need to come to London to find decent work so that I could send money home to my family. I also found myself telling him about St Bride's and Nellie Franny and our love of the Irish language. If I was boring him he was too polite to let on.

I listened to him as he spoke of his passion for art and architecture; how London's buildings enthralled him. And how a young life of privilege had both restricted him and given him many opportunities. But his vivid blue eyes dulled as he explained how his father had made sure he wouldn't experience the horrors of the trenches. Some domestic affairs duty of quiet necessity his father - a buildings advisor to a senior civil servant - was able to produce the adequate paperwork for; a cushioned civil service desk job which, he told me, meant he wasn't even required to register for exemption as a conscientious objector. His father certainly didn't want to risk the whole tribunal thing. Although it did mean he couldn't return to his architectural studies and had to continue living in the family home in Fulham.

His openness made me look within myself and, for the first time, question my own sense of loyalty. Why had I really come to London? Was I running away from something, or the ghost of someone, as Nuala had implied? Maybe I shouldn't have dismissed so easily what she'd said about being needed at home during my own country's struggle. Just like Rory had been. To really give something of myself as my brothers had done, continue to do. Regardless of John's guarded reservations. Only ever wanting me to hear grand tales of heroic endeavours by Irish Volunteers, and our patriots before them, as if bloodshed and terror would always be justified, but somehow, side-lined by valour and silence when it came to me, his sister, a mere woman, wanting to do more.

I didn't know how to respond to the young man; the pain and frustration caught in his lovely voice was obvious. There are plenty of young men who'd jump into his shoes if they could, especially these last couple of years. I wondered if he might want to hear about the situation at home from the perspective of an Irish person. A way to remind myself, is probably closer to the truth of it.

So I told him how I became more interested in Irish politics a year or so before the European war started. I explained about our third attempt at securing Home Rule, which was about to be realized four years ago, just before Belgium was invaded by the Germans. Hearing my own words about my own country ignited a kind of fierce pride which sizzled and spread beneath my skin as I spoke. I told him about the terror of the Bachelor's Walk killings which happened days before the start of the war. He listened carefully then averted his eyes and turned his head to one side as if not wanting me to see his reaction. It's only now occurring to me how tactless I was; he must have been stunned at the image of his own military shooting indiscriminately at innocent people in the streets of Dublin.

But then he asked me if I happened to know any of the victims. I saw no reason not to tell him about our family friend, poor Mr O'Keeffe, a compositor by trade, who had a wife and four beautiful children. The worst thing was that he suffered from his wounds for two months before dying. In the end, there was a grand public funeral for all the victims, I told him. The Irish Volunteers, the Citizen Army, the Fianna, and Cumann na mBan; they were all there in uniform to mourn these innocent people. And because I'll never forget it, I described the hauntingly beautiful music of the Fintan Lalor Pipers who could be heard through the crowded streets, as everyone walked the whole way to Glasnevin cemetery.

He had been listening intently to everything I was saying and I felt as if nobody had ever truly listened to me in the same way. I could have easily continued talking into the late evening, sitting there on that small broken wall, but I was eager to get myself to Fleet Street for the club; just my luck it had been moved to Friday this week. I know I could have simply not turned up but that felt wrong, somehow. I stood up and silently prayed for the school children of the bombed site and imagined their liberated souls entangling their innocence with those who perished in Dublin in 1914, and of course, in 1916.

After a moment, the young man gathered his drawing materials and stood solemnly beside me, thinking his own private thoughts. 'I'm so sorry if I stirred up painful memories of such a traumatic event in your city,' he said, as though he himself might be personally responsible for all of it.

I told him it felt good to remember some of my own recent history, surrounded by today's sadness, such unimaginable horror for both cities.

He moved a tiny bit closer, enough for me to see a small scar above his left eyebrow. A faint aroma of cologne pushed into my nostrils. 'Perhaps you could tell me more, another time, at your own convenience, of course. I mean, I don't presume to think you'd be at all interested in continuing our discussion ...' We both let his words hang in the air between us. His face was beautiful, not a trace of his earlier melancholy, and I knew he wouldn't go without a response, one way or the other, from me.

His name is Edmund. Edmund Churchfield. He could not be any more English if he tried. Even so, we made arrangements to meet again.

I sat on the top deck of the number 15 bus which took me to St Bride's. Seeing the city of London, as the bus trundled into the warm evening, was special; the dusky light held a mysterious charm for me. When I eventually arrived back here, at ten o'clock, I couldn't wait to record today's events.

Secret Acts, Saturday, 22nd June 1918

I thought Nellie Franny would be intrigued to hear my exciting news about the handsome Mr

Edmund Churchfield. Instead, she stayed very quiet and listened with her eyes focused on a multitude of invisible thoughts which seemed to scurry in front of her.

We'd been walking in Green Park. It has become a favourite outing of ours since meeting in the club; one or two joyful hours of gossip and sunshine. But, when I got to the bit where Edmund asked to meet me again, Nellie Franny interrupted me with a gentle hand on my arm. We stopped walking and she asked me directly if I thought meeting an Englishman could be problematic in the future. When I didn't answer, she said she'd noticed a gradual stirring of feeling in me; the sad predicament of our little island, she could see, had been weighing on my mind. Falling for this Edmund, she said, might result in conflict and secrecy. She just stood there in the brilliant sunshine and asked me to reflect carefully on what story of myself I intended to present to Edmund. Nothing about Nellie Franny's tone was hurtful or judgemental; genuine concern, motherly almost, was etched across her forehead as she spoke.

We moved to an empty bench in the shade and as I tried to digest her warning - well, that's what it was, to be honest - she put her arm round my shoulder and said she saw a lot of herself in me and couldn't help wanting to protect me; from what, exactly, she didn't say. And that's why, she said, she had decided to tell me more about her time in this city.

Before the Rising, she did drill practice with a whole load of C na mB girls. Fr McKenna let them use a room in a Catholic school in the East End. Lots of Catholic Halls belonging to the brothers or priests were given to Volunteers and C na mB for their drilling.

Nellie Franny and her friends went to as many Gaelic League concerts and céilís as they could manage. Like now, she said, that had been the main way of meeting and helping London Volunteers. And of course at the G.A.A. matches round London. When she told me she had also played her fair share of camogie in Hampstead Heath, I wanted to tell her I used to play also, back home, but I didn't want to burst into her reminiscence.

It was a grand time for fundraising for the movement; the money, she said, was plentiful when it came to arming the Volunteers. Some of the funds were spent on sending the lads to America to get away from the dreaded British Army conscription for this bloody war with Europe. It's still not safe for any of them to come back, although some have made it back to Ireland.

Nellie Franny paused and closed her eyes as though she was reliving the detail of every memory. A hint of a smile appeared on her face. I wanted to ask her where her young Protestant Matthew fitted into all this. Had she lived in London for long before moving back to Kingstown, and then back here, again? It dawned on me how little about each other's past we knew.

She opened her eyes and put her hand over mine. The furrowed expression returned as she resumed her little talk. The dancing and lectures can't always be separated from the real business of helping the cause. Like me, at first, she was happy to get involved in the cultural and social activities. But at no particular time she could recall, her life became embedded in all manner of dealings for the movement. It had been as natural as moonlight. And just as enticing. I have to admit the couple of céilís Nellie Franny has taken me to in Chandos Hall have made me wonder what it'd be like to assist the Volunteers, here in London. I wasn't born yesterday, I do have a strong inkling as to what actions she and the other women play a crucial role in. Even with the necessary secrecy that goes with their instructions.

So, as things stand with Edmund, I'm not to be surprised if someone associated with the club might expect me to glean information from him. Though what shape that information might take is beyond me, right now. Nellie Franny ended her surprise sermon by reassuring me that she knew I would remain true to myself, no matter what choices I made.

Spanish Flu, Thursday, 18th July 1918

What a groggy haze the last ten or twelve days have been. The weather outside has been claggy and stifling and my room inside has been hot and infected. I hadn't planned on catching the Spanish flu, the new sickness from the trenches so many people have been down with. But it seems to be in every place. And people have actually died from it, Lord God almighty. Not that there's been much about it reported in the newspapers. Not yet, anyway. Like the poisonous virus it is, word of the increasing deaths is being carried in the public air around us. All I know is that Nellie Franny and Edmund have been looking after me, here in Kilburn, surely at their own perilous risk.

At the first sight of my early symptoms, the doctor calmly told me to put away my polishing things, go straight home in the cab ordered and paid for by himself, and stay in bed for a fortnight. He had an instinct I had what he called a mild infection. I can't believe I've been off work all this time. At first, I thought what an extravagant way to respond to a bit of a pale shiver - I even thought herself wheedled her husband into exaggeration - but then that very evening I broke into a river of sweat and began to feel much worse. I didn't have the strength to lift so much as an eyelid, never mind a teaspoon.

I've said before that my employer is a decent person and thank God because last week he sent a messenger with my wages, plus a little extra on top. In his note, he advised very small doses of whiskey, whatever way I could take it, as well as quinine from the pharmacist. All of this, Edmund went out of his way to organize and gently administer, almost daily, as soon as he finished his office work. I wouldn't have blamed him if he ran a mile at the sight of my fever. Especially as nobody seems to know how to stop or cure this virus, except for the very impractical instruction of not allowing yourself to breathe in the same air that everybody else is breathing in.

Gestures of kindness like these I won't forget in a hurry. But what hasn't stayed in my memory during the worst of this feverish illness are the mild ramblings I've been partial to, according to Nellie Franny. She was here with me last night, as she has been most nights, and told me that at least three times, during my general incoherency, I had called out, quite distinctly, for someone called Rory. Somewhat agitated too she said I appeared during these episodes because the person who owned this name didn't seem to be interested in answering my call. She didn't let her curiosity get the better of her by asking me about the mysterious Rory. I'm not so sure I'd be as restrained and respectful of her personal life. Especially as she's already told me about her Matthew, and about her C na mB activities.

What if Edmund was subjected to this impatient hysteria which made me long for my dead sweetheart? A private part of my past I haven't yet shared with him. I'm not ready yet, maybe I'll never be ready. But for all Edmund and Nellie Franny know, Rory could be very much alive and walking around Dublin, or London, unaware of the strange hold he has over me. I only met Edmund last month and this could be an unspoken presence he's not comfortable being around. Dead or alive. It could wreck what we have together. But Rory is still part of me, he's in my bones, I think I want to keep his memory to myself for a bit longer.

I'll leave it for now, maybe wait for Edmund to politely ask me about Rory. If he even has cause to ask me, that is. But like Nellie Franny, it's not his style to pry. Thank God they've taken to each other so well. At this moment in time, I thank the angels and my dear Edmund and Nellie Franny for my recovery. I won't let my thoughts linger on how different things could have been if the doctor hadn't sent me home to my relative quarantine.

Old Men and Boys, Sunday, 4th August 1918

Despite my unfortunate brush with the nasty influenza virus - believe me, I know how lucky I was to get over it - it's true to say my first summer in London continues to beguile me. I am even able to tolerate my grind of a job and isn't that all any Irish girl can expect of her English employment? The doctor's wife flicking her instructions dismissively from her lowered eye lashes and upturned fingers: brass and silver need to be polished, the front steps need to be swept and scrubbed, linens and undergarments need to be laundered. But a lot of my free time is spent with Edmund; we walk; we go to the theatre; we go for picnics.

Our picnics are simple affairs, nothing too elaborate. We've discovered less trodden spots, more tranquil spaces, tucked into the grounds of beautifully designed Christopher Wren churches. One such favourite is a secretly enclosed grassy patch at the back of St Bride's Church on Fleet Street, very close to St Bride's Irish Club. This walled spot is inhabited only by an ancient blood-red rose bush which reaches flamboyantly towards the shifting clouds. Nobody's war has blighted our blossoming relationship, to make torturous demands on us. Not yet, anyway.

But to watch, as we've been doing recently, as troops leave Charing Cross station is torture enough. Their faces emptied of the clear-eyed optimism of previous conscripts, their tired eyes instead reconciled to their individual destinies of victory, defeat, cowardice, who knows what? With all my heart, each time we hold our fleeting vigil on the busy Strand, I pity those soldiers. Each time, Edmund remains solemn and wordless. It's sad to see such old men and boys go to be killed.

The subject of war and conflict is never too far from our discussions, one way or another. During one of our St Bride's Church picnics a few days ago, Edmund was distracted, he seemed entangled in his own thoughts. I watched him as he reached up and touched a thick, thorny stalk of the rose bush, allowing the sharp pricks to cushion into the soft tip of his index finger. 'Do you think those brothers of yours would ever fight in another Irish rebellion?'

Without hesitation, I told him they would be honoured to serve their country again, and again, if it brought liberation sooner. Just then an unbidden picture of Rory flitted across my mind. Would they stay that brave, though, his young face seemed to ask me; I mean, look what happened to me, it could be them, next time. Another rebellion could embed in the flesh of each of your brothers a fatal sniper's bullet. Another rebellion could bury alive each of your brothers beneath a burning building. Or another rebellion could imprison each of your brothers in a fetid cell for a lifetime. Rory's face vanished into the London air as quickly as it had appeared, but not before I realized he was right.

John and Seamus had survived all of it. They were among the arrested Volunteers who only spent a few months last summer in the Welsh prison camp before being released and sent home. I remind myself now how long it had taken for the rest of the prisoners to be put on the steamers back to Ireland.

Edmund didn't notice the thin crack in my stoic assurances about my brothers. He casually moved our talk on to the eccentric Countess and the stories of her flagrant fearlessness in the taking of St. Stephen's Green during the Rising. He was in awe of what he called the true passion and selfless sacrifice of the Irish people. Well, if only he knew the half of it! I have so much to tell Edmund sometimes and I'm glad of it because it keeps me close enough to Rory, a way of not forgetting him, of keeping my loss all to myself.

The other day I read aloud for Edmund a letter from Eamon De Valera. It had been posted from Lewes Prison last year to the mother of John's friend, a young man who had died during the Rising. Edmund listened like a small child captivated by the telling of a revered tale of impossible heroism. He asked me to copy out his favourite line: *Surely that cause must be blessed, for which young men are willing to sacrifice their lives, just budding with the promises of the future, and mothers the fulfilment of the dreams first dreamt by their cradles*. The letter is folded neatly and inserted into the middle pages of this diary. John gave it to me for safekeeping as his friend's mother thought it should remain with her son's Volunteer comrades. Something in Dev's mesmeric words seemed to have forged a strange connection to the idea of a free Ireland, deep within Edmund. I fear there is a great yearning in him to soldier a cause of his own before his troubled guilt engulfs him any further. Is this a blind impulse I should fiercely resist? Should I be dragging him from the notion of worshipping the actions of Volunteers like my two brothers, men he's never met?

Nuala, Wednesday, 29th August 1918

When I got home this evening there was a long letter from Nuala waiting for me. The very last thing I expected to hear from her was the news of her stepping out with a Castle worker. An Irish fella, of course, that I'd have assumed, what with her fierce insistence on no other origin, but a lad working for the Castle government, now that did come as a mild surprise. I thought she hated those uppity office lads; watery and spineless she once described them. He calls himself Niall, a junior clerk of some description Nuala doesn't elaborate on. She does say he's a tower of a young man with golden brown eyes who takes himself and those round him very seriously. Maybe he'll have a calming influence on her fiery theatricalities. But not too calming, I hope, otherwise she wouldn't be the Nuala I know and cherish.

She also told me about Hanna Sheehy Skeffington's secret crossing to Dublin from Liverpool, last month. Having returned from her speaking tour in America, after her husband's murder in the barracks during Easter week, she tried to get a passage home from England. But the Castle wouldn't let her leave Liverpool. So she took matters into her own hands and got herself smuggled home in the hold of a tramp steamship. Nuala said Mrs SS disguised herself by hiding her hair in a cap and wearing a pair of men's dungarees. The black dust from the coal smeared on her face completed her transformation.

I'd already read a bit about her work in the suffrage movement in London and round Ireland. And now, Nuala tells me, instead of being at least tolerated by the Castle, who couldn't bring themselves to welcome her home, she was arrested and thrown into the Bridewell; a squalid prison with the worst of living conditions. As she's done before, she refused food in protest of her innocence.

She was promptly rewarded by being shipped off back here to England to join the Countess and Mrs Clarke in Holloway. Then another hunger strike, another release; my God, this woman has sacrificed so much of herself for her principles, over the years. The government are leaving her stranded in England. She's no longer in prison, but she's not yet allowed back into her own country.

That must have been a very fruitful propaganda tour among our American friends. The government can't bear to stomach the bitter taste of truth coming from such a vibrant voice. A woman's voice too.

I'll reply to Nuala after supper, I wonder how the Volunteers are doing, if she's seen anything of my brothers.

Pleasure in Hyde Park, Saturday, 14th September 1918

I can't believe I'm about to write this down but this afternoon, myself and Edmund had a bit of an intimate encounter under a big, old oak tree in Hyde Park.

We'd been for a long, slow walk through the park. Everybody's mood was ablaze in the hot September sunshine; young families, clerks, nursemaids, and vagrants, all frolicking or basking in the last of the heat, a delicious summer encore.

We decided to cool down under a big, secluded oak tree which threw out lots of soft, dappled shade. We sat with our backs against the cool bark of the tree and let our thoughts drift aimlessly in the sultry atmosphere.

After a few minutes and without saying a word, Edmund moved from my side to where my feet were resting on a raised clump of weedy grass. He proceeded to unlace my walking boots, being careful to loosen the leather before removing each one. I watched, a little bemused, as he rolled down and removed each of my light cotton stockings and stuffed them into my empty boots.

Making sure to keep my long skirt just above my bare ankles, he placed one of my feet in his lap. The other foot I roughly toed into a patch of warm, silken grass in a shady spot along the length of his thigh.

Edmund then encircled my foot in both his hands while watching my face. It felt like a game of some kind, so I played along to the sound of our mutual silence. He slid one of his thumbs firmly down from the ball of my foot along the length of my sole. I jolted my foot away instinctively from the extremely ticklish sensation, a small screech coming from my mouth. But he grabbed my foot once again and, this time, made his thumb rub more slowly, more firmly, all the time securing my toes with the fingers of his other hand, and my ankle and heel within his lap. The motion of the massage shifted into short, fast circular movements, each in turn teasing the warm surface of my skin.

Even though I was sitting down, perfectly anchored to the grass, my balance tipped slightly to one side and I had to claw the soft, green blades with both hands. Not a single word had passed between us. Edmund's smile flipped into my eyes like warm water as he gently, yet rapidly, switched to my other waiting foot. I liked this more emboldened side to him, I was impressed by the new dislodgement in our courting. He repeated the massage, stroke by stroke, not once taking his eyes from mine. My heart was beating as though in my throat. Something intense and visceral pulled and withdrew from an inner, sensual core of my body. All very subtle, all very innocent to a passing stranger, but not for us. Irish Catholic girl, or not, I was totally aware of the effect Edmund's hands were having on me; the impossible luxury of each intimate sensation. I could also see how it was affecting him and I knew neither of us wanted to stop. But just as my breathing became more rapid and my desire for him intensified, I pulled my foot away and brought both knees to beneath my chin.

My smile was wide and wicked. Our naughty game, a prelude of its own, was at an end. For now, anyway.

Lost Souls in Kingstown, Saturday, 12th October 1918

We're beside ourselves in a nervous terror because we have to wait for a reply to Nellie Franny's telegram to her mother in Kingstown.

We were on Kilburn High Road today shopping for a present to send home to young Mary for her birthday, next week. We'd just finished browsing through an array of wooden toys and trinkets in a tiny old fashioned shop. When we stepped outside, with the intention of having a look in the haberdashery shop next door, we couldn't get past a small group of men jammed together on the footpath. They were engrossed in some article they were reading inside the *Irish Independent* newspaper one of them had obviously just bought from the newsstand outside the shop. They had the tired look of railway workers, or dockers. The pale Autumn sunshine pressed into their young skin as they read the article in silent unison. I thought in that moment if they were any of our boys they might have been searching the death notices for names they didn't want to see. Nellie Franny was probably thinking the same thing.

Just as we were managing to squeeze past the men we heard one of them saying that surely all those hundreds of people couldn't have perished so close to Kingstown harbour. The rapid shifting lilt of County Kerry in his voice. We both stopped dead in our tracks and craned our necks to get a look at the open newspaper. The headline at the top of page three pulled us in further:

THE LEINSTER DISASTER.

LIVES LOST GIVEN
NOW AS 451

Five or six people occupying the busy footpath trying to read one newspaper was ridiculous so Nellie Franny grabbed one of the remaining newspapers from the stand and almost tore the thing open.

She just stared at the shape of the headline as though trying to decipher an obscure language. Then her eyes flicked distractedly up and down the columns beneath. She pushed her shaking finger across random, printed words calling out snippets of phrases, a restrained fright in her faltering voice:

... a German submarine attack ... 200 ambulances at Victoria Wharf ... exhausted survivors ... the HMS Lively ... bodies laid out in Kingstown Railway Station ... trying to find relatives ... St Michael's Hospital ... a shortage of beds ... influenza epidemic ... hotels providing clothing, food and shelter ... overcrowded lifeboats capsizing ... people hanging on to the keel ... hundreds of men, women and children jumping into the water ... second torpedo struck the ship ... the vicinity of the mail room ... sea water pouring in from both sides ...

Nellie Franny folded the paper back into shape and placed it under her elbow.

The sky had rearranged itself. Bands of purple cloud had been summoned to lie down and stretch themselves in front of the weakening sun making the light appear lower on the moving bodies of Kilburn's shoppers.

Nellie Franny said no-one she knows had cause to be on the Leinster two days ago, no planned sailings spoken of in recent letters from her family. Even her older brother in Liverpool, who she hardly ever sees, would sail on a different route. The very same for my people, no talk of taking the mail boat. But Nellie Franny grew up and lived for years in Kingstown, she knew many in the harbour town, so she couldn't be certain. She wrung her hands and wondered aloud if we should send a telegram from the post office. The newspaper seller had been listening to us and promptly told us to hurry to the main post office, further up on the High Road, before it shut. He refused payment for the newspaper and wished us and our families the best of good fortune.

All thoughts of young Mary's birthday present vanished. What must be the dying days of this sick war and still people perish, this time by being ripped apart by a torpedo or engulfed by the icy waters of the Irish Sea. I wonder if those Irish boys had cause to send their own telegrams, today.

A Different Dublin, Monday, 21st October 1918

Nuala's latest letter has thrown me a bit. I'm not sure what I should be thinking, or feeling.

Dearest Dervla

I hope this letter finds you well. How is London treating you? Has the ice-cold wife melted a small bit since your last letter? I've heard that St Bride's is a grand club for the London-Irish. They look after their own, which is what I hope your new friend Nellie Franny is doing for you. Although it seems like you've been taking to it well, what with the line you're doing with the new English boyfriend.

Oh, but Dervla, if I'm really honest, I want you to come back home, to Dublin. I think it might be time. Remember your promise that day? Sorry if that's not what you're ready to hear, but there it is, anyway. You know, things are not so full of chaos and gloom these days. Lots of clearing away of all that broken rubble is underway. Some say the ruins will be used in the rebuilding of the streets. Every day the boys are finding a renewed strength in their convictions. Sure weren't you there yourself last year to witness the enormity of the welcome laid out for the prisoners, and for Countess Markievicz herself. They've been elevated to heroes in the eyes of so many who weren't so full of praise for them after the Rising. And I know you're keen to have a flavour of how our little city is, and its new hopes. There's a great anticipation in the air, Dervla. All sorts of talk about who will run for what seats when the general election is called. We could bolster the C na mB ranks and show the boys we're just as good as any man. There's a stronger body of women speaking up for themselves, they're not content to always shadow the decisions of the men. All kinds of lectures on history, as well as the Irish language lessons, are central to the new educational programme in all the branches. If I listen closely, I can sometimes hear your own voice among the women, making itself heard. Well, I know that's silly with you being in London and everything.

Mrs SS was finally allowed home from England after the short spell she did in Holloway. They say it was the hunger strike that struck fear into the authorities. The idea of having to eventually force feed her like poor Thomas Ashe. It'd been the same when she was in the Bridewell. My Niall said that another death like Ashe's would infuriate the world. Especially when you think of Mrs SS's work in America. She told them about the truth of our oppression and about the treatment of prisoners. Her with her very own desperate experience to prove it.

People are noticing more, Dervla. You must feel that yourself in your club. Sure even that new fella of yours seems interested in what's happening in Ireland. Don't tell him too much, though! Ah, I'm only having you on. He sounds very charming. I suppose you've encircled yourself in a bit of London glamour and sure don't you deserve it.

62

Young Mary and your Mam are keeping well, by all accounts. I want you to think about what I've said. There's no shame in returning. You always said you would. It's a different city now.

Your old friend, Nuala

Egyptian Dreams, Sunday, 27th October 1918

Today was one of our Sundays for the British Museum. I saw Nellie Franny waiting for me in the foyer, as usual, and I thought she looked a bit pale. She's definitely lost weight since our last outing. I suppose it might have been the fright of the Leinster tragedy in Kingstown; and the huge relief when the telegram came from her sister telling her that nobody close to them had died. We embraced each other warmly and started our ramble through the beautiful building. We never join one of those guided tours or have a set route planned out; we're happy to just drift through the rooms and artefacts.

Nellie Franny is often drawn towards the ancient Egyptians and their complex burial rituals. It was in this room I told her about Nuala's letter asking me to come back to Ireland.

As we strolled round the mummified exhibits she seemed to carefully weigh and digest all I was saying. When I stopped talking, she surprised me by turning to me and taking my hand in hers. She pressed her finger tips into my palm to get my full attention. She warned me not to dismiss lightly what Nuala said in her letter. She referred to the promise I'd made. She felt it was really important for me to consider not rushing any further into this new life in London if Dublin was where I needed to be. That I also needed to be honest with Edmund if I had any doubts, whatsoever; that life may become more complicated if I don't and it was better to be more open with him now. Weren't these the very things Nellie Franny was trying to warn me about earlier this summer?

But I wasn't to be easily swayed by Nuala's letter, either. Nellie Franny let go of my hand and with the same conviction as before told me that having republican ideals sometimes translates differently when your actual reality is in London. Our beliefs can be altered in the day-to-day compromises we make in our jobs, our relationships. We may grow into different desires and dreams without realizing it. For a moment I wondered which one of us she was talking about.

Alarm bolted through me and I felt as constricted as the sealed up bodies lying, inert, all round us. The exhibits began to look darker and heavier behind their outer tourist-proof barriers. I felt a sudden pulling of myself in different directions. Surely I could somehow give parts of myself here, in London, working with St Bride's, a second home I'd grown close to, and with Nellie Franny; I could get more directly involved in the movement. Edmund could help me, he could even join St Bride's, why not? Yes, of course I miss Dublin but I still feel an immense personal freedom in London. Is that dreadfully selfish of me? Nuala surely knows this from my protracted letters. Would it be so bad to keep half a promise rather than break a full one?

I noticed the light cough Nellie Franny has had these past few weeks was irritating her. She said she needed some fresh air and so we decided to go outside and take a stroll over to the tiny Italian café, opposite the main gates of the museum, to have our coffee.

Ready for Something, Thursday, 7ᵗʰ November 1918

It was our turn this evening to fill the tea urns in the tiny kitchenette in St Bride's. So I grabbed the chance to ask Nellie Franny something I've been thinking about all week.

Earlier, in the main room, the President had chaired a meeting about the imminence of the ending of the war and the subsequent general election. He made special mention of the extraordinary difference the women's vote will make for the Sinn Féin candidates. Breathtaking change is coming, he said, but even more commitment would be demanded.

Afterwards I joined Nellie Franny who was busy with the cups. The aftermath of the meeting had spilled into sub-groups of urgent talk. Ireland's immediate future had once again stirred and settled itself in the eyes and mouths of the members. Nellie Franny seemed to feel the pulse of my nerves as I stood beside her pouring milk into large jugs. 'You better hurry up and tell me what's on your mind before you spill that milk, Dervla Kelly.'

I gave her a rambling speech about now being the time for me to make my mark in the London movement. How the Volunteers were always looking for new decoys so that they could go about their business for Ireland. She had been right that day in Green Park about social and cultural interests not being enough. I was in the middle of explaining that Nuala's letter had been the final trigger when she turned away from her tray of cups and shushed me with her finger on my lips. 'You mustn't let anyone hear you, Dervla, you know that so much of what we do from here is discussed with care and discretion.' Nellie Franny wasn't angry, just cautious and she was right, of course. I whispered that before I made any decisions to go back to Nuala and everything else in Dublin I needed to be more productive here, in London. A city which gave me a kind of neutrality in my mind, a safe space for coming to my own conclusions. It was also the place where Edmund was, but I didn't need to say that to Nellie Franny.

We carried the tea urns, milk and cups out to the side tables in the main room. We took our tea back in the kitchenette as we had our own talk to finish. I made sure my voice couldn't be heard by the other members. Nellie Franny listened as I suggested I could come along with her on her next assignment with a London Volunteer; I would shadow her and fall into any role she thought appropriate. I would accompany her as a secondary decoy to whatever train or bus station, safe house, port, or public building she was required to go to.

'I can see you're ready, Dervla, but you need to be patient. The President will want to do his own checks. I will need to assure him that your Edmund sympathizes with the movement.' She smiled and told me to finish my tea.

Edmund is on our side, that's all the President needs to check. He has shown his commitment to our cause, and to me. I can be patient and I can be careful for Nellie Franny. But how and when I divulge the precise nature of our work to Edmund is more of a delicate undertaking. How delicate, right now, is impossible to know.

Their Armistice, Monday, 11th November 1918

During work this morning, at eleven o'clock precisely, while I was down in the damp basement refilling the metal coal scuttle for the drawing room fire, I heard the guns and bells. That's it then, I thought, as I abandoned my chore, climbed the cold steps, and went outside onto Basil Street. Everyone, everywhere, who had been indoors, rushed out on to the street, and by the gathering sound in the air, all the surrounding roads. There was great, wild excitement. A small huddle of women were crying bitterly, holding on to each other like desperate survivors. It's sad for them, I said to myself, as I stood still in the misty chill and observed the women; their soldiers, sons and husbands who won't be returning home. But I myself felt like a cool spectator, I simply could not join in with the ecstatic street-clogged cheering.

I imagine that Edmund is celebrating with his father at this moment. They had invited me, yet again, for dinner in their house in Fulham this evening, so that myself and Mr Churchfield could finally be acquainted. Edmund joked that his father was beginning to tease him about my actual existence. I made my excuses about having a special lecture night in St Bride's; not totally untrue as tonight was our monthly Monday club, a meeting I don't usually attend. The thought of having to sit in their formal dining room still unnerves me. I'm being irrational, I know, but I'll meet him in my own good time.

I don't begrudge them their hard fought victory - I'm just as sick of the war as everybody else - but it's so very different for me. I only feel glad to think it has to be nearer to my own country's day. For surely Ireland must come now. Hasn't the world shed enough blood?

Nobody went back to work round the city today. There were heaving crowds everywhere. It felt like the whole universe was in central London. I was dismissed from work early and decided to get the tube to the National Gallery for some peace and quiet. As I had expected, the inside of the gallery was almost empty. The paintings seemed dull and meaningless. My journey home this afternoon irritated me, having to listen to some people gloating like over-indulged children. Their war is over, but what about mine? To add to this, and I know this is utterly trivial, I lost the heel of my shoe at Charing Cross while trying to get to the Bakerloo line platform. I felt like screaming like a lunatic at somebody for the stupid inconvenience of having only one shoe intact.

I got home eventually after a long wait on the tube. After my tea, I went all the way back into the city, to St Bride's. It seemed right to show my face. The members are like a family to me, I feel safe round them. I also feel safe round Edmund. I know I've let him down, tonight. It wouldn't have been so bad meeting his father, for Edmund's sake. What message am I sending myself? That Edmund wasn't worth a visit on this momentous day? There was a fair amount of people at the club, each one of them cautious in their talk of the future, and of the imminent general election. Someone said that Nellie Franny had taken ill. I'll see if Edmund can come with me to visit her tomorrow, or the next day. We had a small class in Gaeilge but I couldn't get a bit excited over it with such crowds ranting outside in every place, all going daft.

Later, when I got off my bus near Charing Cross, I saw that some revellers had set fire to all they could get their hands on in Trafalgar Square. And they were singing the most unpatriotic sounding song: 'Knees Up Mother Brown.' As I waited for the tube, yet again, I thought about how so very different we are as neighbouring races. Our grand old Irish songs of glory; none to beat them. It was a long journey home.

The Sound of War, Thursday, 26th December 1918

Just getting to bed now, it's late, I'm freezing and exhausted. I had been feeling so guilty about Nellie Franny because we hadn't seen much of her in the run-up to Christmas. So Edmund and I went to see her after lunch today as we both had a half day from work. We had expected her to be on the mend by now, back to some light duties, and looking forward to the New Year. We were delighted the dreaded Spanish flu had been ruled out by her doctor, weeks ago. Dear Lord, we couldn't have been more wrong about her progress.

She said the doctor told her this morning that he wants her to go into hospital to have routine lung tests carried out. I'm now wondering if he suspects tuberculosis, or pneumonia. I think she's in some kind of denial as she's refusing to go, she has this set idea in her head that she'll get better by herself. The children in the family she works for are very good to her, they bring her food and water, but they are not doctors, they are not even adults, for God's sake.

Edmund brought with him beautiful freesias from Borough Market for Nellie Franny. I saw tears well up in her eyes as she watched him fill a vase and lower the stems into the water for her. He was careful to arrange the purple blooms and place the vase so that she had full view of them from her pillow. His simple attentiveness made me want to throw my arms round him and never let him go. I mustn't let myself take him for granted, I love him too much. I finally persuaded Nellie Franny to let us visit her every evening. I think she was too tired to put up much of a fight and as we were leaving she gave me a spare set of keys. The lady of the house seemed pleased with this arrangement, for now, anyway. We will look after Nellie Franny as best we can. With a bit of gentle persuasion, we might even get her to change her mind about the lung tests.

On our way back towards Charing Cross the streets were filled with noisy revellers out to get a look at President Wilson and the King. It was impossible to avoid the roar and heave of the crowds. The bells of St Martin's Church were triumphant for the President's cavalcade which had started from Charing Cross and was now snaking through Trafalgar Square, on its way to the palace. There were thousands of delirious merrymakers stretched round every street. Each one of them blended in with the endless bunting and flags, which fluttered chaotically in the winter air like a million crazed starlings. Edmund held my hand tightly so we wouldn't get separated. I heard a woman say that twenty thousand soldiers with bayonets lined the route. All the commotion and bustle agitated me, no end. I couldn't even bring myself to smile back at the countless people who squeezed out of the way for us. All I could think about was getting onto the tube.

Outside the station, Edmund put his arms round me and we just stood there, silent, while the whole of central London celebrated as if the world's hardships had dissolved effortlessly into the sky. Edmund finally pulled away and asked me if today's turnout for President Wilson had upset me. He said he knew it must be another reminder for me and Nellie Franny of things at home.

I just looked up at him, my mind a flurry of thoughts about poor, weakening Nellie Franny, and, yes, about Ireland. I tried to explain something which is almost inexplicable. To make him see that the Allies included so many Irish lads, not all of them lucky enough to be returning home. That it will be hard for some in Ireland not to shun them, not to try to humiliate them.

Edmund reassured me that things would settle down and improve now that the war is over. It wasn't unreasonable to hope that because of Sinn Féin's momentous election results Westminster would be forced to put Ireland firmly back on the table. What he said gave me some comfort but my mind is still terribly unsettled. All around me, day after day, I hear the joyous, screeching racket of England at peace, but what Edmund cannot hear is the deafening sound of Ireland suffering its own war, a desperate noise which drills sharply into my heart. I know Nellie Franny hears it too.

I, myself, Wednesday, 29th January 1919

What is it, exactly, that I think I am doing? The freer the world becomes, the lighter our burdens are here, in England. All this while Ireland stands still in a morose darkness I can see clearly, but choose to turn away from by living my life here, in the light. With my English Edmund Churchfield and my English job and my English freedom.

I reason to myself that the new Irish parliament will crank apart the fastened bonds that weld my country to this one. That the astonishing Sinn Féin election results will pave a golden path to full independence. As if it could be that simple. I tell myself that I am a loyal member of my Irish club; a space of sanctuary, a core of identity, my little Ireland. It is a warm, familiar blanket I pull around myself to remind me of my renewed loyalty to my own land; its music, language, culture. And won't I soon prove myself with Nellie Franny as a secret decoy?

But there's a horrible obscenity to it, isn't there?

I am like one of those replica statues in the galleries of plaster casts in the Victoria and Albert museum; unreal and displaced. A sanitized echo of myself. I've often looked at the enormous David and Trajan's Column with Edmund and Nellie Franny. We've joked about the incongruous groupings of the beautiful monuments; the unstained perfection of smooth surfaces never to be smeared over by the sticky fingers of a curious Italian child. All I am is a controlled exhibition of a stand-in version of my original self.

Each day I cradle myself in comfort but wrap nothing around the shoulders of my own people as they wait. And my tender promise to Nuala weighs down on me every night like a thick, grubby cloak.

In the Name of the Women

Ghosts, Wednesday, 5th February 1919

Dear Nellie Franny is dead.

I write this entry in cold shock, my mind is blank with disbelief. I don't understand it, I thought she was beginning to improve a small bit, this past fortnight. We'd noticed tiny perceptible changes. She'd even come round to the idea of having the tests done. I've been by her bedside, wiping her brow and holding her hand for most of the night. I can still see her papery skin translucent over the pale bones and purple veins of her delicate hands. Her long hair streaking wetly across her fevered skin. And now she's gone. Gone. It's too terrible to fathom.

Oh God, to think I had rushed to her yesterday to tell her that Dev and the others are now free. I had been so thrilled and couldn't wait to tell her about their escape from Lincoln Jail. The news, I honestly thought, might give her real strength; the palpable excitement in the club, the wild guesses as to how the prisoners had escaped to a secret safe house. We were going to pray for their swift and safe return to Ireland. Nellie Franny always said how she looked forward to hearing news of the political prisoners, or news of the new Dáil, and the Volunteers. Maybe hearing those intermittent bulletins was the only thing keeping her alive.

When I let myself in at about eight o'clock yesterday evening, I saw that her condition was much worse. The dim air had grown stale round her. Her skin had acquired a deathly pallor in just one day and her breathing was erratic and laboured. I asked her why on earth she hadn't called up to someone in the house to get the doctor. She was too weak to answer me. The expression in her eyes was detached and unfamiliar. I was frantic and shouted outside her door for help. When the family doctor finally arrived after nine o'clock, he told us to leave the room immediately. I found myself pacing up and down the hallway thinking I needed to find a priest.

Nellie Franny's employers skirted round the drawing room door, as if by sending out for their doctor their duty to their foreign maid was somehow fulfilled. I know that's not fair, they've been kind to Nellie Franny. There aren't many who'd let her stay this long in the house without getting any work from her. I'm just as angry with myself for not insisting she go to the hospital like the doctor said she should, weeks ago.

I was too agitated to speak to anyone in the house so I decided to go to the Brompton Oratory, less than half a mile away. Nellie Franny and I have often gone there to listen to the beautiful choir. I had a vague notion in my head that they held a Latin mass in the weekday evenings which meant I might just find someone. A Catholic priest would surely see how desperate I was.

I ran the short distance through the quiet, foggy streets, past the extravagant residences of

Pelham Place, round by Thurloe Square. The thickening fog wrapped itself closely round the sparse green space so that if you didn't know that bit of greenery was there, it wasn't actually there in those moments of that late hour. I know these streets well in daylight but last night every corner and surface seemed to shift through my body. Broken images of Rory's young face began to flitter before me as I moved through the damp air. I found myself reaching out to touch the corner of his mouth, the bone of his cheek. The times we had together leapt into my mind as I got closer to the church. The céilí in Dalkey when we stayed out the whole night, such a clear, clear night. With the dancing in full swing, alone, we rushed out of the hall, past beautiful white washed villas which were nestled and sleeping along Coliemore Road. In the warm stillness of Dillon's Park we sat on a grassy verge in front of the resting sea. That night Dalkey Island loomed like an ancient giant towards us as though to embrace us in its moonlit secrets.

When I returned with Father Darcy, Nellie Franny was unconscious, barely alive. I felt awful. I found myself selfishly thinking of home again, longing to be there with my family. Oh God, forgive me, how could I wish for such a thing? Imagine Nellie Franny's absolute torment, she must have been wishing the same in her last conscious hours. While I held her hand, and soothed her with my voice, recalling our special afternoons in London, my new friend was fading slowly from this world before my eyes, without any of her kin. While Father Darcy gave Nellie Franny the last rites, her employer scurried round in the background muttering a vague plan to wire Nellie Franny's brother in Liverpool. But it was too late, he'd never have made it in time. The doctor had already done all he could, he focused only on trying to make Nellie Franny comfortable. She passed away in her bed in the early hours of this morning. Nellie Franny died knowing her precious country is still unfree.

A Westminster Symbol, Friday, 14th March 1919

I don't think my life will be the same after today; I actually met Countess Markievicz! The woman herself, in the flesh. In Westminster Palace, of all places. When the President asked me yesterday if I wanted the assignment, I didn't flinch. He said he knew he could trust someone who had become close to Nellie Franny. I knew then that she had put my name forward, after all; just as she said she would. To think she's not with me any more is heartbreaking.

Edmund saved me from myself during the past few weeks. I knew he was distraught over Nellie Franny's passing, they had become good friends. But he hardly left my side and when I didn't want to face anyone in St Bride's on those first few Thursdays he begged me to go for Nellie Franny's sake. Do you really think she'd want you to stay away, he'd said to me. On each of those evenings he walked with me to the door of the club on Fleet Street and then came back for me afterwards. Always refusing to come inside. I needed to grieve and remember my dear friend with my own people, he'd said. There would be other opportunities for him to meet the members. But not quite yet. Not at this sad time.

All I've done this past day or so is turn every grain of knowledge and memory over and over in my head. The theory of my life in London, especially the past nine or ten months, suddenly thrown into sharp focus: the passionate lectures and Irish language lessons in the club, recent meetings all over the city about our precious cause, the new work for the Self Determination League - all of it. The gradual embracing, once again, of my own country's fight for liberation. An embrace from London, I know, but isn't this where I find myself? This is my chance to show Nuala and my brothers they can be proud of me.

So now, look at me, I had to accompany the Countess today! Just a day after her release from Holloway Prison.

It didn't feel like it but I must have slept a bit last night. I dreamt of the defiant Countess marching past the guards and keepers, vociferously demanding the ear of David Lloyd George as he made his way to the Commons Chamber, a look of stuffed perplexity on his face as he was forced to stand, speechless, before this formidable woman, the very first to be elected a member of parliament.

Herself didn't press me this morning for an explanation of why I had asked for an early lunch. I remained on my knees, slowly shovelling individual bits of coal into the drawing room grate from the coal scuttle, while I waited for her to consider whether or not 11.45 was an acceptable time to have my break. Both of us, mistress and maid, had been facing in opposite directions - me staring into the virginal flames, still tame enough for my blackened fingers to swiftly rearrange a loose piece of still-solid coal, herself placing a gloved hand on the polished door handle, on her way to the hallway - when my request was granted: of course, no problem, off you go and enjoy your break, dear, don't worry yourself, we'll manage here just fine.

When I turned my head, saying the words thank you very much ma'am, the door had already closed. A curt, almost soundless click. Well, I can tell you, I felt my face flush crimson and I had to stifle an immediate urge to scream through the dustless door that perhaps I'd be late back because I had an important meeting to attend in Westminster Palace with Countess Markievicz, no less, a woman held in the highest esteem in Irish circles, our business was political, and real, and concerned the liberation of Ireland. Most days at work, I have to admit, I wear my invisibility like a slap on the face; the quiet serving girl from Ireland, she won't last too much longer, not now that the war is finally over.

I hadn't a notion how on earth the Countess was going to pick me out in the street. I'd hastily thrown my maid's apron in the odds and ends cupboard in the scullery. But I knew *her* face, so I needn't have worried too much. While I was gazing up at the intricate neo-Gothic architecture of the Houses of Parliament, the low, even voice of an older woman spoke down into the space above my shoulder. 'Even a thing of exquisite beauty can succumb to arrogance and cruelty.' For a second, it felt like the clamouring street hawkers, even the rich tourists, stopped in their tracks and turned to listen to the woman's words.

Recent prison hardship was etched on her pale face and her long woollen coat and day dress hung loosely from her tall, lean frame. But I could see that beneath her plain wide-brimmed hat her dark grey eyes shone like shrouded crystal and the corners of her lips creased in a wry, knowing smile.

'Countess Markievicz, it is a pleasure and an honour to meet you. I am proud to be able to serve you today, just tell me what you need me to do.' I sounded like an over-eager stage actor and I almost bowed. Jesus Christ, *proud to be able to serve you*, what am I saying? I'm making a holy show of myself in this busy street, I remember thinking.

'And I am delighted to meet you also, Dervla. But there's no need for formality, my dear. Thank you for agreeing to accompany me this afternoon. I just need you to make sure we blend, unnoticed, into the tourist groups.' The Countess shook my hand with all the ease of an old family friend. She then took a firm hold of my forearm for support, as we walked slowly towards the grand building opposite Westminster Abbey.

Of course Edmund had taken me on numerous architectural tours in and round the streets and parks of London, but never to the interior of Westminster Palace. He hates when I joke about his father not wanting his son's Irish *cailín* setting foot inside such an important stronghold of the British Empire. A nasty tarnish to his reputation as the Chief Buildings Advisor to the Principal Architect for Parliamentary Estates. Edmund doesn't see the funny side, though.

But today, I have to say it felt mildly unnerving to think that hundreds of officious clerks could be sifting and censoring their way through the civic business of Empire, while perched behind polished mahogany desks, just beyond the many panelled doors which themselves seemed to nestle and observe all movement along the endless corridors.

As we shuffled along with the other tourists, the Countess told me quietly that although she and others did not take their Westminster seats as MPs because of Sinn Féin's refusal to swear an oath of allegiance to the King - this I already knew, of course - she still wanted the small, private pleasure of seeing a symbol of her own political victory before her return to Ireland.

I readied myself for anything. I imagined us being arrested, or at the very least being politely escorted away from the entrance to the Chamber, a flurry of confused embarrassment being tamped down by the addled Speaker of the House as he tried to regain his ceremonial composure.

This symbol, the Countess continued, as we entered the splendid Westminster Hall, its large medieval timber roof looming above us, was her new cloakroom peg in the members' room, which she knew would be there with her name newly printed above it.

I stood absolutely still beneath one of the high, arched windows in the grand hall. I couldn't help lowering my eyes from the enormous roof as I tried to process the Countess's words. I wasn't exactly sure what I'd been expecting, but a thing so banal, so innocuous, had certainly not occurred to me. A cloakroom peg. Hadn't the President stated the Members' Area? Which I presumed to mean the Members' Lobby; I couldn't recall any mention of a cloakroom.

By now, I sensed that the Countess, obviously aware of my blatant hesitation, was carefully studying my expression, my whole demeanour. She leaned closer to my ear. 'I can see from the confused look on your face that this may appear mildly absurd, being what it is. But what I want us both to see is so much more than a plain nameplate. It is a solid emblem for our very future, a simple unblemished vindication of our desperate struggle, which I know will propel me further through my life's destiny of fighting for Irish independence. Whatever the price may be.' She straightened her body and waited for me to say something.

'Oh, please forgive my ignorance, Madame. I didn't mean to appear that way. It's just that I suppose I was expecting something else.' Lame, pathetic words dripping from my lips. Mortification shamed itself into my thoughts and I prayed I hadn't made a complete fool of myself in front of this woman who had already sacrificed so much, suffered more than I could ever imagine.

'Well, why don't you take a look for yourself and then see how you feel?' said the Countess. She offered me a smile which made her crystal eyes sparkle warmly. She was being gracious and forgiving and that made me feel worse.

A few moments later, when we were actually standing in front of the peg in the members' cloakroom, reading the words, Constance Georgine Markievicz, Member of Parliament, St Patrick's Constituency, Dublin, the full impact of her earlier words registered in my mind. Ireland's hour of freedom could be soon. Was it not what I'd been praying for every day? My own country's voice fully liberated at last? Was this even possible within my own lifetime?

I wanted to ask her a hundred questions there and then. For a start, by what drastic means would Westminster be persuaded to truly listen to the newly established parliament in Dublin? Another ill-fated uprising? But I knew she was exhausted and eager to spend time with her sister, Eva, before returning to Ireland.

But the questions came from the Countess herself. 'Let me ask you, Dervla, what is *your* life's destiny? Will you find it here, in London?' She had lowered her voice to a mere whisper, a dulled hoarseness trimming each word.

While we stood there in the long, almost narrow cloakroom, three MPs rushed in and scurried importantly round us, busy with hats, gloves, overcoats, seemingly oblivious to the two female strangers in their midst. Seconds later, they disappeared to whatever parliamentary business waited for them. The weight of the Countess's questions, and the profound symbolism of what she had said in the great hall, leaned heavily on my shoulders; it was as though their mere utterance beckoned the unflinching attention of the other nameplates, of the entire palace itself.

'I really don't know, I suppose I always thought that one day I'd go back to Ireland. That was my original plan of course, but I'm quite happy here in London, for the moment anyway.' My answer disappointed even me. And it was a stinging reminder of my promise to Nuala.

'I see. Well, you have served your country well, child. Today, you have witnessed that which is your inherent right, a withheld treasure you have been unjustly deprived of and you now hunger for its release. I see an outrage in your eyes. Your brothers in Dublin know this injustice all too well.'

It took a long moment for me to digest what I was hearing. My brothers in Dublin; how I missed the sound of their voices and rude laughter. Without doubt, the Countess's words were filled with an impenetrable and utterly familiar truth, but these words also seemed to leak into the air a personal warning which I alone had to decipher for myself. Nellie Franny would examine the intricate fabric on which the Countess's words were finely weaved and help me find my own thread. *Look into your heart, Dervla.*

I thought I might burst into tears at the

mention of my family, so I focused on the emblematic peg once more. Sinn Féin had been victorious in last year's general election, but for me those other names were eclipsed by the one in front of me. When I glanced over at her again, she looked like a creased up version of herself, a new exhaustion seeming to spread through her frail body like the tiny shattered veins in exquisite ceramic.

Although my private life had not been discussed in any great detail, it occurred to me that the Countess must have been informed of Edmund's existence. The English boyfriend whose father had significant parliamentarian connections within his profession. Perhaps, to the Countess, my true republicanism was somehow compromised by my romantic attachment to a young man whose father's only loyalties lay presumably with the King. Yes, this young girl's resolve would have to be put to the test, the Countess's deliberate avoidance of the subject of Edmund seemed to imply. The soft threat of loaded words, unspoken.

When it was time to leave, we made our way quietly out of the building, each lost in our own thoughts. I had totally forgotten to ask if we could view the stunning mosaic work in the Central Lobby, the Commons Chamber, even the blank spaces for the two missing patron saints yet to be beautifully crafted into their waiting panels; all of these things I remembered Edmund describing to me. Instead, we brushed quietly past strangers, ordinary people, who today explored the wondrous palace in a way I now know I never will. Imperialism, its glistening splendour, strangled the beauty my eyes had this morning craved.

During our brief parting outside, the Countess scribbled down the details of a meeting next week of a London-Irish committee for the release of Irish prisoners. She hurriedly pressed the scrap of paper into my hand, the inference being that perhaps I would be interested in attending; the Countess's way of saying goodbye to me.

Before I had time to say anything, she had already disappeared into the lunchtime mass of tourists, newsboys and noisy souvenir hawkers. All I could do was stand still on the pavement surrounded by the smoke and bustle of London and for the longest time I wondered which way I should go to get back to work. How to get anywhere in those moments seemed a total mystery.

I drifted through the rest of the day not really caring about the pull and drag of my Knightsbridge duties. Thank God herself decided to stay out of the house for the afternoon.

A Dangerous Journey, Tuesday, 18th March 1919

Long swirls of damp, red hair escape the pretty woman's cap as she pedals soundlessly along an empty road towards her rendezvous in the quiet hills of a watchful Irish town. The soft contents of the Cumann na mBan depot bag strapped across her chest are packed closely like a new born baby.

Her gut instinct is her only map; to carry an actual map would be treacherous.

Just as the dusky chill bites at her fingertips she slows her bicycle and dismounts in the black shadow of a cluster of huddled drumlins. Here; somewhere here, she whispers into the wet air.

She's been told to bend her head in ignorance if she hears the wheels of a Crossley Tender. With a bit of good fortune the soldiers in a military patrol might spit a lecherous whistle in her direction and continue on their way in their snake tank. She knows what can happen if they have a mind to decelerate.

She cranes every nerve ending in her body to hear the delicate breath of a Volunteer boy. He'll be resting at the bottom of one of the velvet mounds a few yards behind the briary hedgerow beside her walking feet. A leg width's gap in the thorny bushes and she'll be through.

A silent delivery of the most ordinary things his mother probably helped to pack in triplicate this morning: soda bread, hard-boiled eggs, biscuits, woollen socks, cigarettes. This pack doesn't have the weight of bullets or explosives. The women would have cautioned her about such supplies.

I paused and looked up from Nuala's letter.

I'd been dramatizing sections of her latest news from home, for Edmund. Well, interpreting is probably a better word because of course Nuala had to disguise her clandestine military action in the countryside as a dull scene of domestic necessity; a clamorous rush through busy city streets to get essential provisions to her infirm grandmother's bedside.

'Ingenious,' said Edmund. 'So, do you write to Nuala about *me*, your polite Englishman, in the opposite terms to keep a step ahead of the evil censors?' He was just joking, I knew that, but his sudden switch to himself felt a bit like he was dismissing or making trivial Nuala's dangerous journey. Unintentionally, but all the same, a small, irritating feeling, hard to ignore.

'There isn't exactly the need to, Edmund.'

He picked up the teapot and filled our cups with more tea and leaned forward in his chair. We had finished dinner in the big kitchen and he was in no hurry to go home yet.

'So, my love, tell me, what happens next? Does Nuala get to deliver the goods to her needy grandmother-Volunteer boy?' He reached out for the letter but I pulled it back violently and refused to let him read it.

'How would you feel if that was *me* out there in the cold loneliness of sleepless hours on a mission through mountains and hills to get basic supplies to a hungry Volunteer on the run?' A sudden and extravagant question I didn't know I was going to ask; obvious annoyance making itself heard in my raised voice.

Surprise poured itself on to Edmund's face. His eyes shifted awkwardly towards his tea cup while we both sat and waited for his answer.

'Well, to be brutally honest, Dervla, I wouldn't be happy at all. It's like you just said, it'd be dangerous, and full of awful risks.' *Is that all you're going to say*, I wanted to shout out. 'And that's exactly why I'd go with you, on your mission, our mission, to whatever secret ditch or darkened boreen beckoned.'

I smiled for him; a sweet signal to let him know it was a good answer. But I couldn't help feeling it was almost too good, somehow. I mean, would he actually walk out of his cocooned civil service job and take the next mail boat with me to end up God only knows where? Suddenly finding himself in a strange land of whispers and averted eyes at the sound of his English accent. Placing himself in all manner of danger and discomfort because of some chivalrous obligation to protect me against the sudden appearance, out of nowhere, of the British military. Does he think he is infallible to their brute force? That they'd be utter gentlemen and wave us on along the quaint rural patch our bicycles happened to share with the soldiers' patrol? *Better get yourself indoors, sir, it's a late enough hour to be taking the air, off you go now, and be careful to mind the young lass.*

Nuala's letter couldn't be more direct in its reminder of my promise to her; just like each letter she's written these last weeks and months. She won't give up until she sees me step off the gangplank in Kingstown; no return ticket to London. I love her dearly for her patience with my tepid replies of, *yes, my dear, one day very soon, just let me get myself together, there are so many practical things to consider, and then of course there's my beloved Edmund ...*

I scraped my chair against the cold floor and started to tidy away the tea things. I told Edmund

I was too tired to read the rest of Nuala's letter but to be honest I got the impression that he'd already lost interest. While drying the crockery I handed to him he began describing some famous West End restaurant which had wonderful musicians who played the new jazz music during dinner service. He said he'd try and book us a table, perhaps even invite his friends. I was only half listening; my mind shifted back to Nellie Franny, the Countess, Nuala, and my family in Dublin.

Hanna, Saturday, 22nd March 1919

The London-Irish meeting was held yesterday. It was miles away on the tube in north London. A square, windowless hall used for all kinds of community group meetings and events. A trickle of police skirted round, they seemed friendly enough, but quietly alert. Just stand at the back and listen had been the President's simple instructions when I reported back to him last week on the Westminster assignment.

The speakers were eloquent and brave. How I wished Nellie Franny could have been there with me. The other meetings we'd attended together in the club were hugely important, naturally, yet predictable enough in the sweep of their political agendas. This was different.

Hanna Sheehy Skeffington silenced the hall with her vivid account of the incarceration and callous murder of her husband, Francis. Everyone already knew of the tragic events in Portobello Barracks. That along with Francis, two journalists were also shot dead by firing squad; all because of the erratic actions of a volatile and insane officer. But to hear of these murders - there were others too - being retold in the impassioned voice of a woman so dedicated to social justice personalized this endless conflict for the London-Irish in that hall, yesterday. She said she'd been made feel like a criminal, not being allowed back into her own country, while her husband's murderer, in collusion with the government, as she saw it, walked free.

Mrs Sheehy Skeffington, along with Eva Gore Booth, the Countess's sister, also spoke of the work still to be carried out in the crucial campaign for full women's suffrage. How last year's gains excluded all us women under thirty years of age. How they spoke of the rights of women - the shameful list of inequalities - was like a jolt of possibility to the women in the hall. This was our future, you could almost taste it. And weren't these the very injustices supposedly neutralized in the first words of the Easter Proclamation?

Hanna also spoke of English militarism and the plight of political prisoners, on both islands, who were expected to live in dreadful conditions. As I listened I thought once again of my promise to Nuala to return to Dublin when it was time. She was right that day in the tea rooms about me abandoning my own country. Abandoning, such a cold, wrenching word. These days all I hear in St Bride's is talk of more women joining C na mB, more men joining the Volunteers, and others who want a say in the future of Ireland joining Sinn Féin.

I almost feel ashamed of my own freedom, a freedom I've taken for granted, played with, skipped joyfully from one city to another with, even been tormented by like a spoiled child. Forgetting along the way that it could be snatched from me if I dared to say aloud what plenty of others have said before me.

Crossing Over

Poison Letter, Monday, 28th April 1919

What a lovely mass this morning in Maiden Lane. It was in memory of those who died at Easter in 1916. Hearing such solemn words spoken in Gaeilge made it special. It was during Holy Communion that I decided *not* to make Mr Churchfield's acquaintance.

Nearly a week ago, I received a formal written request to meet with him, alone, in his New Fetter Lane offices, near Holborn, in order to discuss the terms of my future relationship with his son. Disbelief would be an understatement if I was to describe my reaction; my hands wouldn't stop shaking as I read over and over what was an outrageous summons from a practical stranger. Jesus, my fears about Edmund's father's attitude towards me, which have been based on pure instinct only, were taunting me through his own written words.

It was Mr Churchfield's genuine desire that Edmund's obvious happiness continue, the boy himself having made it abundantly clear that he had, in me, found his true love. However, the neatly typed words informed me that certain matters pertaining to my general background, family members, education, and current London associates, would require immediate written clarification. Mr Churchfield trusted that I would fully understand the basis of his concerns and that while cultural harmony was naturally the bedrock of his personal philosophy, some differences were unfortunately too great to sustain any type of relationship, romantic or otherwise.

The obvious delicacy of his request would undoubtedly be met with my utmost discretion and compliance, he felt assured. The concluding paragraph contained a final instruction to me for the inclusion of a detailed account of my involvement, however small or domestic, with the newly formed Irish Self Determination League, and the so-called St Bride's Irish Club.

I'd always known that my polite refusals to have dinner at Edmund's family home would worry him, sooner or later. I simply needed more time to prepare myself. The idea of meeting his father had always unnerved me for reasons I still can't explain to myself, never mind to Edmund. And now this shocking letter.

I'm fairly sure I could live with Mr Churchfield's patronizing superiority, his arrogance, and his weakly disguised anti-Irish views, all of which I must have been subconsciously anticipating. But what riles me about his sly letter is the sense of implied authority behind his clinically written words. The thinly veiled assertion of cosy fraternal, military influence with friends of friends in places like Dublin Castle.

Even so, why on this earth would my family background, such as it is, interest someone like Mr Churchfield? I don't have any particular interest in *his* siblings or personal interests.

Although I have no intention of replying to the letter, its hidden threats have been playing on my mind since its arrival. So, I suppose it came as no surprise earlier this evening when Edmund asked me if everything was okay. We'd been strolling along the Southbank, watching the tourists and traders as they bought and sold ephemeral memories of London. Edmund suddenly stopped walking and took up both my hands in his. A confusion of questions raced through his eyes. 'You seem a bit distracted, Dervla. These past few days you haven't been your usual self, tell me, what is it? You do still love me, my darling, don't you?' Mild alarm had ripped at the edge of his voice.

How could I tell him about his father's toxic letter? It would certainly be an act of selfishness on my part. Besides, I didn't want to risk losing Edmund. What if the unthinkable happened and he sided with his father? Instead, I told him that of course I still loved him, it was just that I'd been missing my family recently. Perhaps, I said, I'd arrange a late summer crossing on the mail boat, a short trip which would do me good; the idea itself came to me in that same moment. Yes, it was time to see my family, it would be my first trip back since my arrival in England.

I placed my hands on his beautiful face, telling him I'd always love him. This simple declaration of my eternal love for Edmund I will never betray. And because of his love for his father, I also know I'll never show him that vile letter.

Jazz, Sunday, 4th May 1919

What an evening I've had with Edmund; it blurred and blended in strange ways. I've only just said goodbye to him.

We went to a private dancing place called Ciro's. It's on Orange Street behind the National Gallery. It's kind of like a fine dining restaurant for high society types. The plush entrance has large ionic pillars and inside there's a small floor space for dancing in front of the music stage. The entire room is decorated in a very French looking style with mirrored glass walls and dark wooden panels. Edmund's friend, Charlie, said it had been used as a hospital at the end of the war.

Yes, I finally got to meet the famous Charlie, Edmund's officer friend who was injured in the war. A charmingly polite and solemn man. I had begun to think he didn't actually exist. His fiancée, Helena, was with him, a delightful woman whom I got on very well with. She wore a loose black chiffon and embroidered dress which added to her natural beauty. I've been looking forward to meeting some more of Edmund's friends, especially Charlie, as Edmund speaks of him with such admiration. Edmund rarely moves in what he calls his social circle so I hardly know anyone in it. Not like Dublin where you see your friends most weeks. I do miss the simplicity of bumping into people in the street and having a gossipy chat about nothing in particular.

A small band of musicians played the new jazz sound I've been hearing about. It seems a whole world away from the céilí music I'm so used to, but I think maybe I'll grow to like it.

I was a bit nervous using the heavy silver. Silly really, I know, but I'm usually polishing it, not eating with it in such an elegant place. I couldn't tell you the actual name of the dish I had, the entire menu was in French. But it consisted of the softest chicken flavoured with a rich, beefy gravy. The potatoes were thinly sliced and covered in a well-seasoned creamy sauce. The entire meal was exquisite and served by immaculate young boys wearing long, starched aprons. The others were totally at ease and I wondered if Edmund had already told them I worked in service.

At first, the music didn't make much sense to me, I couldn't feel a steady rhythm or follow any kind of order. Edmund said that was deliberate in the composition of some of these pieces. Over the past couple of years he's bought some American recordings for his gramophone which he's promised we'd listen to together. The sudden little curved blasts and small booms of the wind instruments were just part of the whole thing. Later, people danced wildly with an abandon I didn't think possible in a place like that. The dance floor heaved and sighed to the tinny clash and soft thump of this new jazz.

So many society girls smoking cigarettes from long holders and drinking champagne as they cast their smiling eyes round the room. And when they danced with their handsome partners, their glistening pearls swirled round their slim bodies like flamboyant strings. I simply could not take my eyes off them! Their silk chiffon dresses were fashioned in the new drop waist style I'd seen in Harper's Bazaar. The satin and beaded fabric of the necklines circled and draped against their pale skin. I had attached a beautiful trim of jade silk round the neckline and sleeves of my own black and grey cotton chiffon tea dress which Helena had admired when we were introduced. Some girls had their hair cut in the daring new bob style. And the luxury of long, heavy fur-trimmed coats strewn across the narrow shoulders of young women who sashayed into the restaurant like jubilant blood sisters.

Helena saw me watching the girls and said I had the face for a short waved style and offered to take me to her hairdressing salon. I thanked her saying maybe we could do that one day soon. I didn't tell her Nellie Franny used to try a lot of the new styles with my hair. I even let her cut inches off it a couple of times. My lovely Nellie Franny; I still miss her so much.

I think after dinner Edmund and I really wanted to dance but we felt too shy to join in with the dancers. I knew I'd be too self-conscious with the new steps, which was mildly ridiculous, actually, as it wasn't as if we were shy together in other ways; things have moved on since our daring little flirtation in Hyde Park, all those months ago. We did want to wait until we got married but, in the end, those resolutions were discarded. I may have let Edmund think he was my first, I know that's not fair but, well, he didn't seem to want to know. He still doesn't.

Charlie's shrapnel injury which shattered his ankle had put an end to his dancing days and brought him home from the war. Understandably, he didn't seem keen to elaborate on the story. Instead, the four of us sipped wine and watched the glamourous couples. Some of them slotted together seamlessly as the tempo increased, a boundless intimacy propelling their swift movements. We sat back and enjoyed the music, it was like having our very own London stage show.

A peculiar thing happened just as the clarinet player finished his enthralling solo. Edmund stood up to go to the bathroom when, out of nowhere, a middle aged man appeared and seemed to push his shoulder roughly into Edmund's back. Edmund was startled and turned to face the man who then placed his hands on Edmund's arms, as though to steady him, and apologized profusely. Charlie made to stand up beside Edmund, a quietly automatic response, but Helena grabbed his sleeve, pulling him back into his chair.

It was more the sound of the man's voice, his accent, a distinct and very polite Dublin lilt, which made me stare up at his face. His carefully combed hair, the riotous applause, and the flicker of low lamp light distracted me at first, but then I felt sure I recognized him as one of the S.D. League members who is often in the club. One of the three or four men who are always close by the President, like shadows, especially when he addresses us, or gives a lecture. Jesus Christ, was there some truth in what Nellie Franny said that day in Green Park? That I'd be expected to use Edmund in some way.

There was something about the way the man held onto the side of Edmund's arms, his bone-tipped knuckles gripping the soft, woollen fabric of his spring coat, that made me decide not to address him in a familiar way. I thought it better to say nothing, not because it wasn't my place to speak, but because in that moment I saw two separate parts of my life standing in front of me, each carrying its own meaning, its own set of personal behaviours. Each so different to the other. Nellie Franny had been the only club or League member known to Edmund, in person. The encounter ended in seconds and was forgotten by the time the band started their next piece.

But thinking it over now in my head, the other peculiar thing was when the man released his grip on Edmund, he turned his head, quite slowly, to acknowledge me. In doing so, he gave me an intense look, an odd sort of lingering stare which was neither friendly, nor rude. I'm glad Edmund didn't notice the man's stare and I'm glad I said nothing, to either of them.

A Proposal, Tuesday, 6th May 1919

Well, that's it now, I can't quite believe it but tonight I actually asked Edmund to come back to Ireland with me after Christmas. Such a simple, obvious thing. Why in God's name hadn't I thought of asking him before now? A new life together, in Dublin. All I can do now is wait for his answer.

What a week it's been for me. I've been to Palmer's Green to distribute handbills for the S.D. League; over two evenings I had more than six hundred new names to submit to the League. Nellie Franny would have been proud of me. I was exhausted by the end of two separate public meetings. But I felt inspired and productive. The Countess's words, still entrenched in my heart, gave me all the strength I needed to keep going. There were hundreds of London-Irish and countless League members in attendance. You couldn't miss the interspersed men in khaki; as if a single London Volunteer would let himself stand out in the crowd. No-one gave the police, or the soldiers, reason to assert their authority.

More than once, I found myself wondering if Mr Churchfield had somehow commanded a gormless junior clerk from the Estates office to slither inconspicuously in and around the edges of the crowds in an attempt to leech scraps of crucial intelligence, which would, instantaneously, in his tiny odd mind, incriminate me in the eyes of the British establishment; the efficient removal of his son's beloved, yet most undesirably Irish, *cailín* would naturally follow. I know he is Edmund's father but I hate that man and everything he stands for, and now I hope I never have to lay eyes on him. What I wouldn't say to him. How dare he try to probe into my private life, my beliefs, my family background.

And what exactly does he think he knows about the League? Has he ever taken a stand on wrongly imprisoned patriots who simply want recognition and true liberation for their own country? Has he ever read one of the League's pamphlets about the need to educate people here, in England, on what is happening in Ireland, about our rich Irish language, history and literature? Has he even heard of our wonderful G.A.A., or any other Irish organizations for that matter? I doubt it. The detestable Mr Churchfield is more likely to be one of those imperial types I hear the club members talking about; men who flaunt their shameful ignorance by offering casual, armchair support for the frequent raids, arrests and deportations that have so many times been the consequences of League membership.

All of these thoughts and questions had been flying round inside my head this evening and before I knew what I was saying I just blurted out my idea to Edmund. We were having tea in the big kitchen downstairs. The other lodgers were either out, or in their rooms. Every word I said to him was true. My heart felt as if it was being dissected and I was the one holding the scalpel. If I've frightened him away it's my own doing entirely.

I can still see the look of amazement in his eyes when I told him that I wanted us both to move to Ireland early next year. At first, he said nothing at all, he just looked at me for a long moment, a myriad of unsaid responses crowding his shocked face. Then, with wide searching eyes, questions tumbled from his mouth: 'You want to go back to Ireland? And for me to come with you? But, darling, what job would I do in Ireland? How on earth would we live?'

I hadn't really formulated in my mind how the conversation would run in reality. I told him we'd find a way, that at first we could live with my family for a few weeks. He could have one of my brother's rooms, they're barely in the house these days if Mary's letters are anything to go by. It'd be unusual, yes, especially with us not actually being married, but, well, it'd put our own future into context, we could make more definite plans.

'But Dervla, how would I explain such a decision to my father?' There had been a note of irritation in his voice when he said that. This annoyed me but I tried to hide the impatience in my own voice.

I said that we'd simply tell his father together, and that when he saw how much we were in love, he would surely understand that we were determined to be happy, no matter where we lived.

'But you have yet to meet my father, Dervla. How do you propose we so easily tell him? This could break his heart. Why not spend some time in his company, then we could think about the best way to broach the subject?' I knew it was a logical, sensible suggestion. He watched me refusing to tell him so.

Instead I just sat there at the tea-stained wooden table, desperate for him to really hear what I was saying, rather than worrying about what his father might, or might not, feel. So I decided it was the perfect time to tell him about meeting the Countess, our brief visit to the Palace of Westminster, and about the London-Irish meeting for the prisoners. But not about this week's activities, I didn't want to overwhelm him.

He listened intently. It was easy to sit there, as the evening drew in around us, and open up my heart to him. I told him that spending time with the Countess, listening to her sister, Eva, and to Hanna Sheehy Skeffington, the absolute passion in their voices when they spoke of independence and equality and social justice, made real and personal sense to me. 'Tell me, how can I stay here knowing that my own country is still shackled to another?'

He moved his chair closer to mine and slowly smoothed my hair back from my face. His warm finger tips caressed my forehead and temples. A new tiredness had touched the skin under his eyes. 'I understand the powerful effect these events have had on you, my love, truly, I do. But what exactly would you yourself achieve by going back? Don't you like our little life here, in London?'

I heard my voice rising as I answered him. 'Perhaps I will achieve nothing, Edmund. But I know it is somehow my duty to try. Of course, at first, it will be difficult, and I admit it scares me a bit, but I know we'll manage. I have to find my *own* niche, and I want you by my side. And yes, I will be sad to leave London, but by staying here another year or two, I will be a million times sadder.' Now was the time to remind Edmund of his own compassion for Ireland's plight. 'You've said so many times how you empathize with my country's pain, how you can see the injustice. When my family and friends see for themselves that you share my conviction, they will love and support you, they will welcome you as a true friend of Ireland.'

'But what of my being English? Surely, I will never be accepted in Dublin?'

'Believe me,' I said, 'those who are fighting for Ireland's freedom need all the support they can get. And sure lots of sympathizers and activists - take the Countess, for example - were born in England. Right now, the members in St Bride's speak of little else but Ireland's liberation, especially since the new parliament. You and I could really help in that struggle.'

I could see he was trying to digest everything I was saying as he stared into a future which must have appeared desperately foreign to him.

'Dervla, you are the centre of my life, I love you so much. Hearing your devotion to Ireland's cause makes me really want to say yes to you, to do something useful and right, but ....' When he trailed off like that, being so close to saying yes, I was even more determined to persuade him, but I could see something else was pressing on his mind. I pleaded with him to just say out loud whatever it was he was thinking.

He looked away from me and stood up. He took a few slow steps towards the kitchen sink by the window. I could see the pale glow of anonymous lamps flickering in the darkened houses beyond the dusty glass. He remained standing with his back to me, his left hand rubbing the back of his neck. I wondered if he shared this mannerism with his father, if there was any physical resemblance between the two of them.

'It's just I suppose I feel that such a huge decision would be a cruel betrayal of my father. I so want to make him proud of me. You see, he has plans for me to join his advisory business, or if not, for me to work my way up through the civil service here, in England.'

'But what about your *own* plans, Edmund? You always talk of leaving your safe civil service job and finishing your studies in architecture. Maybe you could do that in Dublin?'

He turned from the window to face me, a terrible agony in his eyes. 'Dervla, I owe my father my life. Don't forget he kept me out of the trenches. He would simply see my going to Ireland - a place of conflict with England - as an awful insult to himself. Don't you see my dilemma?'

A heavy blackness charged to the front of my thoughts. I took a deep breath and shoved the weight of it away. I made my words come out slowly: 'I can see how loyal you are to your father, Edmund, and I respect that. But I also see how that loyalty could wrench *us* apart.' In that moment, it struck me that by refusing to tell Edmund about his father's interrogation letter, not only was I lying by omission, but I myself was perhaps sealing our fate. A fate partly determined by the implicit contents of a letter I am still trying to fully decipher. To show the letter to Edmund could seriously compromise our love for each other. At the very least, it would damage his relationship with his father. Either price is high. But by not taking the risk, I could pay an even higher price.

'Listen to me, Dervla, I would never let that happen. I just need some time to get my head round everything you've said.'

It tears at my heart when I think about what I've asked him to do for me. As I sit here writing this entry, for all my brave talk earlier, I wonder if I will ever live in my beautiful city again. Because right now, I cannot imagine my world without Edmund.

Peace Circus, Saturday, 19th July 1919

That stupid Peace Holiday today did nothing but unsettle me. All of these gatherings of extreme jubilation nudge me further outside of my life. I knew Mr Churchfield picked up on my unease. Oh, sweet, sweet Edmund, why did I agree to meet your father today, of all days? All those people waving wildly like identical participants in a strange ritual, its primal chant shared only by their initiated souls.

I will never forget the look of sublime pride - pride only an Englishman in England could possess - which emanated towards me from Edmund's glistening eyes. It almost broke my heart, the two of us standing there in the crazed bedlam close to Whitehall. As if something insidious was poisoning the balmy air all around us and only I could smell it. Edmund offered his eyes and smile to me like an excited child through the ecstatic crowd; he nodded and willed a complicit response from me. I strained all my effort to appear impressed, but behind it I wanted to scream out in rage at him, and his father. I broke quickly from his gaze, but he didn't seem to notice my state of apathy with all the happy chaos around us. Neither did he notice the hurt it was causing me.

But his father noticed, I'm sure of it. It maddens me now to think that, having avoided meeting this bigot for a whole year, when I was finally confronted with him in the middle of a vulgar circus, he saw me at my most vulnerable. All his suspicions, whatever they were, finally confirmed. For Edmund's sake, I was courteous and respectful to Mr Churchfield, but the truth is I couldn't stand being in his presence. Not a trace of his son about him, thank God. His perfect Saville Row suit couldn't make up for his watery eyes, his mechanical smile, or his damp-skinned hand shake. He took great pleasure in listing off for my benefit what countries were parading past us. As if I couldn't work it out for myself. His hateful letter, of course, remained tactfully unmentioned.

Edmund wouldn't accept any excuse from me all this week for not coming. Surely I understood the need to celebrate such collective freedom, he had calmly reasoned. It was the only time he didn't acknowledge, even in some small conciliatory way, the ongoing occupation of Ireland. Has he suddenly forgotten? And what about our plans, why hasn't he spoken to his father yet about coming to Dublin with me? It's all we've been talking about for the last two months. Finally getting him to consider an extended trip next January to see how he felt was a small triumph for me, only a few weeks ago. Maybe I should just be done with it and book a one-way ticket for my upcoming passage home. I know I don't mean that, it's just that all this indecision is bloody maddening. The doctor and his wife have finally agreed to give me a few days' leave during August and September so I suppose this short trip will give us time apart to think about what we really want.

Edmund has loved the carnivalized London air ever since the ending of that terrible war last year. It was the only air he inhaled during those vicious years but for that he will always feel guilty. Of course I'm glad he didn't have to fight in the trenches for the British army. Perhaps I am a hypocrite. But as for today's Peace Holiday, I know in my heart that I tried very hard for Edmund.

I admired the national colours of the long procession through central London. The French looked stunning. I thought Commander-in-Chief Foch looked fine on horseback. The Australians and Americans were very impressive. Those representing the Liverpools and Dublins were only too familiar to me. For me to accuse those

Irish boys of some kind of patriotic suicide is futile. I saw in their hardened eyes - the ones without any other option - the justification for feeding their families by battling one alien enemy on behalf of another.

Two Cities, Sunday, 31st August 1919

I was almost deranged with torment as the mail steamer left Kingstown harbour early this August morning, taking me back to England, and to Edmund. I just stood there, motionless, my hands gripping the thin railings, like so many displaced people before me, crossing the same water, and I wished I was immediately back in Dublin city. Back to myself, finally. Back to my family, Nuala, my streets, my beautiful, confined streets. Not much has changed, but everything is different. Republicanism has thickened the Dublin air. Ordinary, everyday life bracing itself.

How wonderful it was to be reunited with my mother and sister, and dear, outlandish Nuala. An extra sparkle danced in her eyes when she told me all about her new Niall. Well, not so new, of course, I realized when she reminded me she'd met him this time last year. It's a pity I didn't get to meet him while I was home, to see for myself if he's good enough for my precious Nuala.

She seems besotted with him, so I'm happy for her. But I couldn't resist telling her I never expected her to let herself fall for a Castle worker. He's a sympathizer, apparently, and he keeps his head down at work. Some of the other Irish clerks avoid all talk of politics amongst themselves. At first, Nuala and Niall didn't talk much about her C na mB membership, or the S.F. clubs, they were far too busy falling hopelessly in love. But as the weeks and months went by, she said, they opened up more to each other. He told her of his plans to leave the Castle to take up a printing apprenticeship. He was going to join the Volunteers and prove his commitment to the struggle for independence. That's a lot of planning, I remember thinking, but kept it to myself. No, I have to say, I'm thrilled for Nuala, she's a fairly good judge of character, and she deserves this blossoming new happiness.

My mother told me that quiet, urgent activities were now taking place in our house; like countless others, it has become a safe house. Her day is often measured out in units of what, or who, needs to be hidden, and for what period of time. It wasn't the right moment to casually announce the likelihood of Edmund sharing the boys' room with Volunteers on the run; I've yet to tell my mother about our future plans, never mind burdening her with such an incongruous image.

*

The whole time of my leave home, I was dreading the thought of that tired, old train shunting and snaking its hefty carriages back through the Welsh countryside, towards the grime and fog of Euston Station. And the prospect of having to return to a boring job I've grown to hate.

On the steamer this morning it also occurred to me how London air is full of something stifling, almost choking. Oh, the difference, Good old Dublin, I love you, I heard my tiny voice telling the diminishing coastline of south Dublin; Nuala must have gotten to me, too. This spoken expression of love disarmed me, it was so simple, so revealing. What on earth am I doing, I wondered? So that was the exact moment, there and then on the mail boat, I decided to return to my beloved city, sooner rather than later, with or without Edmund. I'm still not sure if making him actually choose between me and his father, as Nuala advised, is fair. Either way, it's time to admit to myself that Mr Churchfield will probably get what he wants. Which means that horrible man may win his petty war with me.

Nuala was disgusted when I told her about his nasty letter. She said that the entire business reeked of something ominous and if it was her, she'd put as much distance as possible between herself and that pompous Mr Churchfield. Which of course, up until very recently, had been exactly what I was doing. It was a great relief to unburden myself with Nuala, to really vent my anger and hurt. I made her promise not to say a word to anyone about the letter. Too incendiary were its contents were they to be divulged in the wrong circles. For now, my mind has filed the letter under the paranoid delusions of a small-minded man.

*

I wish I'd had more time with Nuala. I can't believe it's been nearly two years since we saw each other. I suppose our letters have filled many gaps in that time. I didn't get to tell her about last month's Peace Holiday in London. How disjointed and out of place I'd felt. How I wished she'd been with me during the mayhem and cruelty of that day; I wouldn't have felt so exposed in front of Mr Churchfield.

But I did make sure to tell her it was now time for me to act, to do my bit for our movement, just like she'd always wanted me to. That I'd start in London under the instruction of the President. Then I'd begin planning my return, for good. No more half promises. She wrapped her arms round me and said she had always known she'd have to wait but every day she had prayed for me to decide for myself.

When she let go of me there were tears in her eyes. I told her I had to do things in stages, that I didn't yet have an actual date, but all being well with Edmund, it'd be in the New Year. *All being well with Edmund*; I knew I was trying to convince myself, as well as Nuala. She fixed me with an intense, proud gaze. 'I know in the core of my bones, girl, you'll be back in Dublin sooner. You are needed now, or as close to now as humanly possible.' I suppose this cemented things in my mind this morning.

I peeled myself away from her green eyes, their hypnotic truth almost goading me. All I could think was how on earth I was going to convince Edmund that we needed to start planning now.

And that literally meant uprooting our lives in London to enter a war in Dublin. His demons offering themselves to him in the colours of my Irish flag. Is there a better time for him to embrace a cause, a thing he has pined for these past few years? By all accounts, the situation is getting worse up and down the country. My country. Can he do this for me?

We'll be waiting for you were Nuala's final words to me.

*

It wasn't the only decision I made on my trip. Even though I was exhausted from the return crossing today, I found my way to Fleet Street from Euston Station. I couldn't wait until Thursday and I remembered the monthly meeting had been moved to this evening for some reason or other. Just as well as I was desperate to talk to the President. I felt totally ready for some kind of act of duty, an assignment I could make my mark with, and I needed solid guidance from him.

I needn't have worried as the President must have seen a torment in my face when I walked into the main room. He broke away from a few members and ushered me quietly into a small office space. Standing opposite him, alone, with the door closed behind him felt like a slightly odd thing; I'd only ever been in his presence in the main room with the other members, or with men like the one I recognized in the jazz restaurant. Now, he seemed smaller than usual, more fragile, like a kindly older uncle. After he'd listened to me lament my absence from Ireland, how I missed my family and how I desperately wanted to do more than distribute handbills and attend meetings, do something that would directly help the cause, he sat down at a makeshift desk and retrieved a ledger of some kind from a pile of his personal papers. He swiftly flicked to a page containing a neatly written numbered list. He looked up at me for what felt like long, quiet seconds, a pensive charge behind his bright eyes. Then, matter-of-factly, he asked, 'How quickly can you sew a heavy cloth of segmented lining into the woollen overcoat I've often seen you wearing in cooler weather?'

I knew immediately why he asked this question. My mind raced with anticipation as I told him I'd need less than one week.

Crossing Over, Thursday, 11th September 1919

Invisibility was my plan. To remain seated in a hidden corner with just enough distance between myself and the other second class passengers; especially the small huddles of British troops I was told would be here and there sitting, playing cards, and sleeping.

If the military decided to stop and search me, a lone female traveller, at either Holyhead or Kingstown, all I had to do was make an elaborate show of the delicate silk camisoles which were wrapped in layers of white muslin inside the canvas satchel which was part of my small hand luggage: *Such a beautifully lasting fabric, personally chosen in Harrods by my good lady mistress. She'll have no-one else, but me, make the simple camisoles for her well-to-do lady friends in Ballsbridge. What an amount of money she spends, what with my travelling expenses, and naturally she pays me for my time, all because she doesn't trust the postal service.* I even had names and addresses memorized in case someone asked for details. All in all, a sufficient distraction.

There were less soldiers in the main second class saloon than I had expected. In fact, there weren't many anywhere on the ship. The ideal situation to hope for the President had said when he told me to book the early morning passage; most people would be quietly resting. I could smell the previous night's kitchen meals clinging to the air as I walked slowly round the passenger seating, outside the saloon, looking for an empty area. Avoid coming into contact with small children, or anyone with drink taken; the President's brief, practised words echoing in my mind as I held the lapels of my heavier than usual coat. The very last thing I wanted was someone falling clumsily against any part of my lower body, a note of curious surprise arriving in their eyes.

So strange to think of that first crossing I had taken between Kingstown and Holyhead, during the war, never really paying a lot of attention to the military on board; all on their way to their next posting, or going on leave between the two ports. Every one of them a target for the German U-boats. Their different accents, the almost dismissed fear of a torpedo strike, it all just blended as part of the war itself, an enormous horror ordinary people on the mail boat had no control over, no say in at all. Everybody knew the dangers, listened to the warnings, but stepped on to the gangplank, regardless. Even after the awful fate of the Leinster, only weeks before the war ended, with so many lost souls at the hands of the Germans. But there were new jobs to find in England, there still are, and that's all there was to it. That war was a war of other nations. People took their chances on the crossings.

Now of course, I was part of another, much closer war, one that had never stopped. And the sight of British soldiers on the ship was a menacing sign of that war still being fought on my own dear land. The U-boats were gone but what had replaced them was more destructive than the threat of a sudden submarine strike.

As I walked towards the middle of the steamer, I passed by English and Irish soldiers laughing amiably and talking together, off duty and relaxed. I was close enough to smell the tobacco and fried dinners pressed into their khaki. Too close, I quickly realized. So I continued on until I found a small section with a few rows of almost empty wooden seats which curved slightly sideways, away from most of the other passengers. I sat down carefully and guessed I was somewhere near those big smoky funnels which, when you watch them from land on a dismal day, seem to shiver and cower from the moody force of the elements.

A gentle lull had descended everywhere, and apart from one or two cranky children, only the subdued exchanges between the soldiers could be heard. An off-duty postal worker sat reading a newspaper in the half predawn light one row in front of the one I had found for myself.

I thanked God for the calm sailing conditions that morning. I envied the passengers who spent most of the crossing out on deck. The huge expanse of infinite sea would have been enchanting. To breathe in the fresh new day and imagine the stilled secrets submerged forever beneath the surface. To watch out for the ghostly white letters of the Kish lightship, a welcome signal that Kingstown harbour was not far beyond.

Instead I sat like a statue in my hard seat, the tell-tale signs of this path I seem to have chosen for myself sitting inert and cool against the inside fabric of my coat. I had concise instructions as to the destination of the guns I was smuggling across the Irish Sea, but more than that I didn't know. I tried to will the minutes to speed ahead but thoughts of the life I might have had, instead of this one, crept into my head.

But it was a life which was stolen from me and, for the shortest of times, from Rory. The baby we'd made that perfect summer night in the secluded park in Dalkey; the whispering breeze letting us catch the distant sound of the dance we'd hurried from, its ecstatic rhythm thudding on the balmy air. Then, two months before what would be our last Christmas together, the secret death of our secret baby. Early pregnancy stomach cramps I told myself; didn't every woman suffer one way or another while carrying her baby? But when the late night bleeding started, the cramps got much, much worse. I was too ashamed to leave my bedroom, or to call out to my family for help. Hours before, they had left me to my early night, Mary saying she'd bunk in with Mam to give me a bit of peace.

Barely a word passed between Mam and I the next morning when I told her my baby had disappeared in the night. It seemed pointless, no, it was insulting, somehow, to tell her Rory had already proposed, that we'd been planning to tell her any day now. After she'd removed the bloodied chamber pot, she prepared hot soup for me and sent Mary with a message to my work. She stayed in the house a while and left through the back door when a doctor I'd never seen before came into my room to make sure I didn't have an infection after my *unfortunate trouble*. His words. When he left the house I just lay on my soiled bed, my insides burning. Why had my body deceived me? When Mam came back she walked into my room and placed fresh, clean sheets and a newly bought towel on the chair beside my bed. Without looking at me directly, she reached out and put her hand on my shoulder. I didn't want her to leave my side but I knew she had to for her own reasons, one of them a clenched shame which might reveal itself to me in her pained expression.

So if things had turned out differently, if those cramps hadn't been so severe - did I look after myself properly? - I would have been somewhere else, sleeping soundly beside a dreaming child, not on this early morning mail boat. The only tragedy of that life being that my child would have still grown up without his or her rebel father.

I was very careful to keep my long coat fully buttoned and tucked loosely round my legs, not to drag any part of it on the floor, or allow it to lie across the seating, the danger being that the concealed Webley hand guns may have revealed a little of their revolver shape if sitting flat on any surface. For a long time, I remained totally upright against the back panel and held my hands clasped securely together to stop them from shaking.

I knew that six Webley revolvers would need rounds of ammunition but the President said I wasn't ready to carry any more than the short handguns. Fear would stiffen my whole body, enough to draw the wrong kind of attention. He said that next time, we would see. It had taken us almost an hour to position the revolvers snugly inside my newly altered overcoat: two at either side, two at the back. Six hidden pockets, expertly stitched, placed deep inside strong double lining. Shin level.

After about forty minutes I became aware of two men walking amiably into the curve, towards my row of seating. I saw their khaki before I saw their faces. 'This nice young lady won't mind if we take these seats next to her, will she?'

The voice of the soldier who spoke startled me but I covered my fright with a friendly smile and some small words of casual agreement: yes, of course you can take the seats, sure isn't there plenty of room for the three of us to stretch out.

'Thank you, miss, we're just looking for some peace and quiet away from the lads, so don't mind us.' They draped their uniformed limbs into the hard wood seating a few feet to my right.

My body sat itself up even straighter, my hands gathered my collar round my neck. The rehearsed words assembled themselves nervously in my dry throat: the silk bought in Harrods, the handmade camisoles, the well-connected ladies in leafy Ballsbridge. My fingers brushed over the canvas satchel which lay like a waiting life jacket by my side; ready for use but hoping it wouldn't be required. If they decided to search me and found my six bulletless guns, I hadn't a hope of saving myself.

I was almost disappointed when neither of them - one from Liverpool, one from Dublin - said another word to me. Not even a soldierly glance of mild curiosity at my hand luggage. Or my carefully buttoned, weighted overcoat.

They spoke quietly to each other about their families, and about next Christmas. Ordinary daily life. A replica of shared conversation, no doubt, between others just like them, like me, who sat in second class wooden rows, just like ours, on the fated Leinster last year.

The entire action was easy to carry out. Bloody terrifying, but easy.

*

121

So now, as you have probably gathered, my heart is mobilized, every fibre of my being pulls me back to Dublin. I am needed there. When I finally arrived home, later that first morning, my family was thrilled to see me so soon again. Mam didn't ask me for any more details when I told her about the camisole delivery to my club's Volunteer contact near Westland Row. It didn't surprise me to learn that the house continues to be a safe house. Now even more so than before. It was inevitable; everyone's a republican in Dublin. I need to get used to calling the Volunteers by their new name, the Irish Republican Army.

That evening, Nuala came with me to Central Branch of Cumann na mBan, where I renewed my membership. We were instructed to stay for the arms handling class. We learned how to clean, hold, empty, and load a rifle. Most of us were fairly used to handling the much smaller revolvers by now. The Captain told me that when I was home for good I'd learn how to use these weapons. A practical skill for the women whose job it was to support the men at any given moment.

*

The other main thing to report from my second trip home is of course my brief reunion with John. There was so much that needed to be said, which didn't get said, stuff that may linger in the lost space between us like a roaming ghost without a place to rest. But it was a good start, at least, and I know he must have risked so much to come to the house and spend what little time we did have together.

Earlier, I had been in Nuala's house where she introduced me to the famous Niall. Something about him, I can't put my finger on it, exactly, but I sensed a kind of hollowness in his character; I don't know, it's been a strange few days, I suppose, maybe I just don't think anyone is good enough for Nuala. Anyway, when I got back to the house to get some rest before making the trip to the Kingstown mail boat, wasn't John sitting there in the half light of the front room, the curtains fully drawn against the late afternoon. Quiet as an obedient child, his hands spread flat on the table, his eyes on the door as I walked into the room.

I was surprised but how wonderful it was to see him, my older brother, sitting there watching and waiting for me. He stood up and embraced me tightly. I had to breathe back the tears and regrets and shared sorrows and focus on the joy of our reunion. A faint smell of hair pomade and cigarettes coated the collar of his old tweed jacket. I've tried to record here as much of our talk as I can remember. It felt important somehow to get it down on paper. Before I have to get rid of my diary, for good.

John, thank God you're okay. It's not safe for you here.

Don't worry about me. When I heard you were home I was determined to see you. Sorry I didn't get to see you

last month. How come you're back again, so soon?
St Bride's sent me over with some stuff to deliver. It's
okay, it's all done now. I'm sailing back late tonight,
I'll go straight to work in Knightsbridge in the morning.
No-one knew I was coming this time, not even Mam. It
was much better that way.

I see. I didn't realize you were that involved in your
club. What about your Englishman, what does he
make of your activities?

Edmund is on our side, he supports the movement.

Does he know why you're back in Dublin, now? How
much have you told him about the things we need to do
for the movement?

He knows enough.

Did you make sure not to act suspiciously on the
crossing? They're hauling people in for the slightest
thing.

I'm here, aren't I?

I just worry for your safety, Dervla. The fact that you're
the sister of two Rising Volunteers on the run gives the
military suspicion enough.

But that can't be helped, John. You had nothing to do
with me joining Cumann na mBan before, or with me
being a member in St Bride's now. I've made my own
choices and I know how to look after myself.

They've been watching men wherever they can, trying to work out who's joined the provisional government's new army. But we're not making it easy for them.

I'm coming back to Dublin for good, John. It'll be soon and Edmund's coming with me. I'll tell Mam, tonight.

But would you not stay in London a bit longer, now that the European war is finally over? You've made a good life over there with Edmund.

We love each other, John. And I love my country. Why can't I have both at the same time? This is where I need to be and Edmund wants what I want.

I see.

Like you, I have a duty to carry out. Being in London has opened my eyes to that duty.

I might as well tell you then that this house has been used as a safe house a few times. Mainly sheltering men for a night or two. They make themselves invisible. We don't want to burden Mam but she's offered our room a hundred times. We try our best to see her as much as we can, which isn't often, I know.

Mam told me about the house last month. Everyone it seems wants to do their bit. And I'll protect Mam and Mary when I get home, they know I will.

We spoke of more but I can't recall the details now, I'm still exhausted from the trip. John said

Seamus got called away by Mick Collins at the last moment, otherwise he would have come to the house with John to see me. I know that must have been a wrench for Seamus.

People say time is a great healer. I've come to believe that time, or the lack of it, forces acceptance for some pain that needs to heal. Perhaps it's the same thing. Anyway, a kind of acceptance is what I felt when the time came for John to leave through the back door.

*

Some members in St Bride's are talking about the R.I.C. planning to take on new recruits from England, war veterans and other ex-servicemen. The talk is that there will be advertisements for men who are willing to help the British restore law and order in Ireland. They talk about law and order - their law, their order, while ours has been trampled on for years. Do they know what history means?

There have been reports of robbing and plundering by soldiers in the town of Fermoy, in Cork, twice this week. I've also heard that some of our boys were shot by the military in Inchicore. And all Sinn Féins were raided according to the members. Could any of this even be possible? Everything is happening so quickly. The idea that there will be even more military presence in Ireland - these war veterans - fills me with dread, but also with a new resolve. I need to save as much money as possible to bring home with me. I have to finish this long entry now as it feels like lead is pressing down on my eyelids.

Hang the Strikers, Sunday, 5th October 1919

My hand is shaking in solid anger as I try to write these words.

We were on our way back from the Palace Theatre - Edmund was given free tickets to *Monsieur Beaucaire* - when I suddenly found myself in the middle of a horrible argument in the street with some unhinged woman who, shouting at anyone who cared to listen, compared the recent strikers with dirty Irish, or German cowards; shot and hanged she wanted them to be. Her absolute ignorance about ordinary struggling people made my blood lurch. But to hear the hatred in her voice, the way she spoke of Irish people, stopped me dead in my tracks.

Edmund tried his best to usher me away, saying she was probably drunk, but I pulled my arm loose from his grip. I turned to the woman and demanded to know if she had any sons or friends in the military who at this moment were murdering innocent civilians all over Ireland. It was a futile question and the look of dazed confusion on the woman's face almost made me laugh out loud.

My pen is calming me, I don't feel so furious now. Perhaps it's because today was also the day when the railway strike actually ended. People everywhere are excited and relieved, they can move round the land again. I feel the same because today I was able to buy my one-way train ticket to Holyhead.

Tomorrow, I will tell Edmund what he already knows. For the second time this year my heart breaks. First, poor Nellie Franny's awful death, now I have to tell my beloved I am leaving England next month. Because I doubt he will be ready or willing to come with me in the New Year, even for the trial period we agreed. So why prolong the heartache? God knows, I've done enough waiting.

A Vision of Me, Sunday, 2nd November 1919

My journey home to Dublin draws closer. Soon this life of mine in London will exist for me only in the shape of memories. Staying at Edmund's house last night was one I'll cherish.

A kind of polite diplomacy has been hovering between us these past few weeks. Edmund's been saying the right things about joining me soon. Very soon. Insisting that nothing at all has changed in that respect. Last night, while we sat on the settee in the drawing room sipping brandy in front of a blazing fire, he told me he'd already begun his research into how he might take up a position in the public buildings service in Dublin Castle. The very system of control and rule we at home want to dismantle and make our own. The irony was not lost on me; I'm sure he felt it too.

We were listening to the American jazz recordings he'd promised to play on his gramophone for me. Being in his house late at night, with his father away on business, felt very different to being there during the day. The room shimmered in the firelight and two turquoise tiffany table lamps cast soft, dome-shaped glows on the walls. Silvered candlelight flickered, illuminating the crystal decanters and glasses which sat on the old, Dutch drinks tray. The heavy burgundy velvet curtains and two armchairs, even the chopped wood on the hearth, seemed to enfold us within the heat of the fire as the swirling sounds of the Original Dixieland Jazz Band punctuated the air round us. I thought back to the night in the private club when I was mesmerized by the beautiful society girls as they danced with a frivolous abandon I envied.

Maybe it was the mild burning intoxication of the expensive brandy that made me kick off my shoes and haul Edmund up to dance with me. I made him take off his shoes so that his father's oriental rug didn't get scuffed. The expensive weave felt soft beneath my silk stockinged toes. We tried our own version of the jazz dance steps, adding little flourishes as the melody surged and jumped. We laughed at our clumsiness but it didn't feel awkward. The rug was the perfect stage for our amateur dance moves - I've no idea if they even have proper names yet - and I have to say it felt good to be held and twirled in his arms.

When we'd danced to both sides of the recordings, Edmund took my hand and sat me back down on the settee. From the mahogany bureau in the corner he quickly retrieved a sketch pad and charcoal pencils and placed them on the low table in front of me. He took off his jacket and tie and flung them on to the back of one of the armchairs. He rolled up his shirt sleeves and took a few sips of brandy from his glass. He picked up the pad and charcoal and sat down on the other armchair. 'I want to draw you, Dervla,' he declared, still slightly breathless from our dancing. 'I know I've never really drawn the human form before, but it feels right, tonight, that I should try. Would you mind terribly if I tried to sketch something of you?'

I couldn't resist his smiling enthusiasm and besides the evening was becoming infused with a sense of bold spontaneity. To sit as Edmund's model would be intriguing. I've always admired the architectural sketches of London's beautiful buildings he keeps in his father's study but it never occurred to me he'd want to create a drawing of me. Why had I never asked him before?

I'm not sure what came over me but I decided to surprise him by stripping down to my undergarments. I wasn't being salacious, I just wanted him to capture this version of me, without the obstruction of layers of embroidered linen. But more than that, I wanted him to see me, to singe me into his memory; my eyes, my neck, my shoulders, the heat-brushed skin of me. This, perhaps, one of our last, precious evenings together. On this side of the water, anyway.

'You are quite beautiful, Dervla.' Already, he'd fallen into an intense concentration, the sudden lack of outer clothing apparently unnoticed. 'A beautiful face full of contradictions and secrets, this may take some time, my love.' A flash of a smile. Maybe he sees more of me, after all, I thought, smiling back.

The room shifted and settled around our silence. The heady aroma of brandy wafted from the two glasses on the small table. The only sounds were the sparked spit and resettling of burning wood. And the soft, waxy sweep of charcoal on thick paper. The heat from the fire kept my bare skin warm as I watched Edmund work studiously. His expression was one of singular contentment, vocation-like. He was immersed in the form emerging in front of him. When one of the thin straps of my silk camisole slipped from my shoulder, Edmund motioned with a blackened finger for me to leave it where it had fallen.

Camisoles. I let my thoughts drift back to September when I had those hand guns placed so carefully inside the lining of my coat. The rehearsed story about the beautiful silk camisoles packed in my canvas bag, ready for their wealthy Dublin ladies. The one Edmund now sketched started its journey by my side - a silk distraction - on that mail boat. I longed to tell him about the sailing. To talk about the heavy metal cargo I concealed. To explain my reasons, if they could be put into words an Englishman could fathom. It would be a test of his conviction to my cause. Of his love for me. Would he walk across the line I'd already crossed? Would he sacrifice the comforts of his homeland to help liberate mine?

But the words didn't want to enter the cozy drawing room. Deceit, of course, was easier. To risk killing our love, our uncertain future, was too much. So I pushed away the secrets etched on my face and coveted the quiet intimacy of our artistic exchange. I would have sat there for hours for him.

For one long moment Edmund just stared at his work, self-criticism lining his forehead. I thought for a second he might tear the paper to shreds in sheer frustration and fling his efforts into the fire. Flushed, he hastily opened the top buttons of his shirt, smearing charcoal on the front of the white fabric with his fingers. He moved further back in the chair and seemed to relax more as he continued his work with a renewed vigour.

When he finished he ripped the sheet from the pad and brought the drawing to me. He offered it, solemnly, his dusty fingers clutching the sides as though presenting me with a piece of his own flesh, for my approval. 'You can be honest, Dervla, say if you hate it.'

A portrait of me. A softly sculpted, idealized rendering of me. More Botticelli than Picasso for sure. I was looking at an impossible vision of myself. A flawlessness that even the thick charcoal couldn't diminish. An impenetrable near-porcelain mask, all secrets finger-smeared away. This pleased me. Edmund was just as determined to preserve the evening as I was. No sharpened life creases would be permitted. I admired his obvious talent and told him I absolutely loved it.

I propped the portrait gently against the silk-covered cushion on Edmund's armchair. She remained there, a shy voyeur, and observed as we sat on the settee and held each other, skin touching skin, the topography of one so different to that of the other.

Dublin

To open the front door tonight to my brothers holding up between them a blood-soaked Volunteer seized me in fright. It was far from the emotional reunion I'd expected since my return from London.

The lad was about seventeen and petrified in his terrible shock. Mam swiftly moved me to one side and guided the three of them in through the front room. I checked outside for a sign or shape of unwanted attention; nothing but the hushed brown brick and concrete presence of the other terraces standing sentinel. I stepped back inside, closed the door, and followed the others.

I now know why a worn mattress and a thick stack of old newspapers are stored upright against the wall in the narrow side room behind the front room; a once cramped space which now seems to have a new use. I watched from the door frame as my mother and brothers helped the boy to lie on the mattress which Seamus had pushed down on to the floor. John carefully removed the boot from the boy's left foot. The immediate task was to stop the flow of blood from what looked like a gunshot wound on his lower leg. Mam instructed John and Seamus to fetch tea-cloths and small towels from the hot press, as well as the filled kettle of hot water over the fire. My job was to bring the bottle of brandy and first-aid box we keep under the sink in the scullery.

My first-aid skills came back to me but it was my mother who did most of the work. I did my best to keep the boy calm and insisted he drink a few sips of the brandy while my mother compressed his wound. His name was Pat and he gripped my hand as the blood from his leg saturated the newspaper covering the mattress. He hardly said a word and I knew better than to ask him how he got injured - I guessed a failed ambush, or a visit from the authorities – and there was no time for talking, anyway.

John and Seamus said they'd be back as soon as they could for Pat; they needed to borrow a motor car to take him to the nuns in the Mater Hospital. I was relieved as I knew the best would be done for him while they waited for a doctor to examine him properly. I prayed it was just a flesh wound and that Pat's shock wasn't too severe. The only help we could give him was to clean his wound with the water and alcohol and tightly pack the leg and wait until the car came. We were securing the last of the bandage when we heard the front door close; I'd have to wait for my warm homecoming embrace from my brothers. My mother told me to sit on the floor and keep Pat awake and comfortable while she disposed of the bloodied papers. She then made tea and insisted Pat eat some bread and ham before the boys came back.

Our young patient began to come back to himself. The alarm in his eyes had subsided and he spoke of his parents and the boys in his Battalion. I tasted the brandy in my teacup and smiled at my mother who sat on a tiny stool by Pat's side, opposite me. My thoughts drifted back to the last time I'd had brandy; an expensive bottle served in crystal tumblers while Edmund worked on my portrait in his father's beautiful Fulham drawing room.

When the lads came back three hours later our work was swift and careful. Pat, flanked by my brothers, hobbled outside and was gently guided away from our house and down the hill to the waiting motor car. Their movements were soundless. We had been told to close and lock the front door without delay. My mother didn't ask where John and Seamus would sleep tonight.

I had it in me to recover from the sight and state of young Pat clinging to my brothers in our doorway, a frightened I.R.A. boy depending on my family to help stem the rebel blood from his leg. I chose this path for myself, for this country. I asked Edmund last year to make the same choice and so far all I have for an answer is his absence. It occurs to me now that my mother and John and Seamus, now that they have me back home by their side, may be wondering if Edmund will have it in him to help shelter and feed others like Pat. If he will be committed enough to sever his own bonds and join us, as he keeps promising, in our Irish struggle against his English nation.

Raid, Friday, 26th March 1920

The horrible sound of a window being smashed through woke the three of us at 4.00am. Mam was on the landing before me and Mary. She was holding a lamp, alert, as though she'd been waiting there for hours. We ran down the stairs, almost stumbling over each other, to find bits of broken glass on the floor in the front room. We just stood there, wordless, in the pale glow of the lamp, staring at the shards. Our silence was interrupted by a loud hammering on the front door. An English accent followed; something about the tone was oddly farcical. 'If you don't let us in this moment we'll break down this door.' Mam gave me the lamp to hold. It was the military, she told us, her voice calm as she walked into the hallway. We rushed after her but she had her hand on the latch, already calculating the cost of the broken window, a new front door impossible to afford. The burden of it lying across her curved shoulders as she unbolted the door with her other hand.

We had received intelligence from one of Mick Collins's Castle boys only two days ago that this might happen to a house on our terrace. Our orders were to quickly pass on the contents of the tiny dump we'd been building up since last year. What with C na mB being suppressed and driven underground with the other nationalist organizations months ago, it was a small miracle I managed to get hold of a member so quickly to help me. Using two sacks, we transferred revolvers, maps, lists of enemy addresses, and handbills to another friendly house, in Rathmines.

The officer in charge was very young, and very polite, almost gentlemanly. His raised his eyes towards the ceiling like an actor before rehearsal, waiting for the lines to form; hard to imagine him as the window-breaking, commanding type. But of course you could never really tell with the military. The three soldiers who accompanied him stood in a casual semi-circle round the three of us, their rifles resting but ready, a collective menace in their glassy eyes.

'Mrs Kelly, please excuse the excessively early hour. We are here under orders from Dublin Castle to conduct a search of this house.' There was a marbly flourish to his pronouncement.

'You'll not find anything here, there's just us women and we want no trouble,' said my mother. A different tone in her voice to what I had expected; assured and a little hardened. Her chin held high to the officer's declaration.

'You're to leave my mam alone, mister, she hasn't done anything,' said Mary. Her arm moved instinctively to shield our mother. The soldiers' semi-circle tightened round us. I grabbed Mary's wrist and tried to pull her behind me. A sour smell of stale cigarettes coated my face as a soldier reached out and placed his hand on Mary's shoulder. The officer sighed dramatically and cleared his throat and his soldiers backed away lazily. One of them, the tallest of the three, smiled his indifference to the signal.

'If you would simply allow us to do our job, ladies, we will be out of your way in no time. Perhaps one of you could light another lamp, or two.' He may not have looked much like an officer but at least he could control his men.

I had been going over in my head what I would say when they asked us where my brothers were. *My two brothers, you are joking, aren't you? Sure I haven't laid eyes on either of them in months. I'm only just back from working in England, myself. Last I heard, they'd both got jobs off down in West Cork. Sure you know yourself what young fellas are like when they get a notion to take themselves off somewhere.*

'What exactly are you looking for at this hour of the night, officer?' I said.

'Ah, you must be the daughter, *Dervla* Kelly. If you don't mind, I would like to ask you some questions, please.' He turned to his men and instructed them to start searching the house, except for one room: my bedroom upstairs.

The officer looked at the lit lamp I was still holding and motioned for me to lead the way up the stairs. He assured my mother over his shoulder we would only be a brief moment. 'Don't be distressed, Madam, we'll be back downstairs in a jiffy.'

My mother rushed towards the bottom step but an outstretched rifle poked its barrel through the banister and blocked her way.

'I'll be fine, Mam, you stay with Mary.' I turned away from her and continued up the stairs.

When we were inside the room I now share with Mary, the officer closed the door quietly behind him. The dim light softened his youthful face even more, so that he might have been mistaken for a shy grammar school boy, playing at being an important army officer. Was he suddenly nervous? His shoulders appeared too wide for his small stature and he was at a loss as to where to place himself. He opted for resting his hand on the door knob, as if to immediately run from the room. Then his earlier politeness spread itself into unlikely questions about my life in London: did I miss being there? did I miss my friends? did I like working in the big city? Unnerved but intrigued, I wondered why would the military be bothered about my time in London, and not the whereabouts of my rebel brothers? Was he playing with me, trying to catch me out, did they actually suspect something about me smuggling the revolvers from England, last summer?

But he barely listened to what I said, he didn't take notes or appear to retain the bland details of my neutral answers. And before I knew it, he had opened the door and we were walking back down the stairs. I decided not to tell my mother about his questions, no point in alarming her, she'll have assumed it was about her sons.

Under the watchful eye of the officer, the soldiers spent two hours slowly removing loose floor boards and half emptying cupboards and drawers as they searched for guns and papers that weren't there. Not any more.

When they were finished the officer turned to me and actually thanked me for my time. He offered a gracious smile towards my mother's averted eyes, but didn't go as far as apologizing for the mess, or the broken window. When it was clear that she had nothing to say to him, he led his men, empty-handed, out of the house.

While we carefully put our scattered

possessions and upturned furniture back in order, I could sense Mam covering her relief for young Mary's sake. Making out like it was an obvious mistake of identity; mixed up addresses and names. That the soldiers themselves were too embarrassed to even break into pieces a single floor board which wasn't already easily taken up. They had no idea who or what it was they were after. Mary went along with it, but the look in her eyes was one belonging to an older child, one who had already heard and seen what adults can be driven to if pushed far enough. She didn't contradict my mother with the fact that the officer had addressed us with the correct names. Still, she had prepared her young self. She, like our mother, had stood straight and proud, ready to say nothing about John and Seamus.

Afterwards, we quietly busied ourselves with an early breakfast. I saw then that fear and anger had left the house with the soldiers. I noticed how calmly my mother resumed her small, daily activities. This is what we put our mothers through; it is what they have become used to. Which also makes me think that maybe this wasn't my mother's first visit from the military. That, without my brothers' knowledge, perhaps even as Mary has slept soundly upstairs, my mother has endured other intimidations in her own home. All while her adult children have been disappearing and running, or enjoying a nice life in London.

I came back upstairs and retrieved my diary from the secret panel beside the fireplace, here in the bedroom, the one room the officer wasn't interested in searching. I sat down on the floor and started to write this entry. What kind of instructions had that officer received? Now that I'm back home I need to be much more careful.

God, how I miss my dear Edmund. The wrench of our goodbye two weeks after he made that lovely portrait of me was almost too much to bear. He would be appalled and ashamed if he knew how we were treated earlier this morning, in our own house, in our own city. But of course, he doesn't know all there is to know about this house, and about me. I never did get round to telling him.

It all feels so wrong, Edmund in England, me here in Dublin. His last letter was full of grand platitudes promising that any day now his father would relent and give us his full blessing; it'd mean a proper date could be set for the crossing. But I know the truth of it is that Edmund is being forced to make a simple choice: an unsavoury existence in Dublin with the Irish girl, or a secure and privileged life in London with his father. Come on, Edmund, I need you to make your decision; come to me, or be forever suffocated by your father.

Death of a Magistrate, Saturday, 27th March 1920

This is the Dublin I've returned to. A real and bloodied quickening of the pulse which has been thrumming through the pale flesh of our tormented streets.

I've just rushed home from an errand to tell

Mam what I heard outside the Castle gates. A group of office clerks were in a fever of talk about a gang of men who they said had dragged some important magistrate off a tram near Merrion, yesterday morning. The men surrounded him on the footpath, there and then, in broad daylight, and shot him three times in the head. According to the clerks, the passengers were screaming and some of them tried to help the man as pools of his blood reddened the ground where he lay.

Mam said she already knew about yesterday's shooting.

Instead of asking her how she knew, I asked her, carefully, if she thought John or Seamus were in any way involved. A direct question which, had I still been in London, would have been an intrusion into a world where the right to ask such things had to be earned. Even about the manoeuvres of your own family. But I am here now, back in Dublin, earning that right as more republicans seek out not only the quiet lanes and rural shadows of this conflict, but also the teeming city spaces of our capital. Same enemy, new tactics.

Mam looked at me as though reading my thoughts. 'I don't know everything my children are involved in, not the precise detail of what's required of them. But I do know that, like plenty of mothers, necessary secrets are kept from me.' It was the best answer my question was going to get.

I sit here and think it out objectively through my mother's eyes. Yesterday, before dawn, a military officer takes her daughter upstairs for a quiet chat while his soldiers conduct their half-hearted raid. Later the same morning, a magistrate is assassinated in cold blood while her two sons are, once again, like many of their Volunteer friends, on the run.

I see a devoted mother who doesn't need to know everything because to know everything is to know too much. I see a mother with a younger child, another daughter, to consider before she herself, three or four or five years from now, will carry her own secrets, walk with her own shadows, in the name of whichever cause seeks her out.

Brief Note: Nuala, Sunday, 28th March 1920

Another Easter approaches; more painful memories of those who were slaughtered in Kilmainham. No wonder Nuala doesn't seem herself this past week or so. Either that or she's not as enamoured with Niall as she's making out. Fiercely proud, that woman is; I know not to probe too much where her burning romance is concerned.

Although I thought she'd have taken more of an interest this morning in Dillon's when I told her about the attack on the house and the strange little boy-officer's questions about my time in London. I couldn't help but notice a slow shift in her mood as I was describing what happened; dismissive, impatient, almost. A slice of annoyance in her voice, too. Why was I making an elaborate story out of it when we're all to expect our houses to be raided a multitude of times, she'd wanted to know. *An elaborate story.* I wasn't exactly expecting an armful of pity, but a modicum of concern wouldn't have gone amiss.

With a tight shake of her head she refused the second cup of tea I offered to pour into her cup. I knew she'd become more evasive, perhaps even fall into some sort of lovelorn sulk, if I didn't drop the subject. So I tried to catch her eye and suggested we plan to see a play or two in the Abbey, just like the old days. 'Remember, Nuala, we had a theatre month, about three years ago, when we saw *Fox and Geese*, that witty little play by the two women writers? And the other play, the one by Shaw?'

Her expression softened slightly with the memory. '*Man and Superman*,' she said, coolly, not looking over at me. I knew I wasn't going to get any more chat out of her and decided to try the idea on her another time. We left the tearooms soon afterwards.

Unquiet Streets, Sunday, 4th April 1920

During the fourth anniversary of Easter 1916 the military gave a great display of holding up and searching everybody who came into or left the city. They fear another rising. This time more people will play their part, are playing their part. All income tax papers were destroyed. The clerical confusion of it will weaken the Castle. And 150 police barracks were burned down round the country by the I.R.A.. I have less and less time to write what I want in this diary. Better that way. I'll have to dispose of it soon enough, anyway. Thank God I got some paid work taking in sewing jobs; at least I can be close to my family for a good bit of the time. Nobody knows what the Castle is planning for our city.

And I haven't received a letter from Edmund in weeks, not since before the raid. Jesus Christ, the raid, that officer's strange questioning about me being in London; have Edmund's recent letters to me been destroyed?

Cordon, Tuesday, 13th April 1920

These hard streets belong to Mary as much as the rest of us.

She wants to understand for herself why prisoners are starving themselves and a general strike has workers taking to the streets in sympathy with them. This is her war too and she needs to discover it in her own way; I know that. I remind myself she's a thirteen year old girl who's been reared in a house full of nationalists; each of us, at different times, trying to shield her young ears and eyes from the talk and blood of this fight with the English.

I stopped myself from dragging her back home through the thickening crowd outside Mountjoy Prison, today. *Give her the space*, I said to myself. Mary must have known I'd spotted her from my position opposite the main outer gates; there wasn't a sign of truancy about her movements. She was with a small group of friends, girls her own age. They were putting together one of the makeshift cordons at the far end of the road for the public protest which had been descending outside the prison. An older C na mB member was supervising them as they worked swiftly at the edge of the swelling crowd.

Mary knows I've been mobilized on various days at Mountjoy since the hunger strike started last week. She's been listening to me telling Mam about the Dublin branches displaying themselves in proud, military ranks outside the gaol. How a huge number of women of all ages have been kneeling down on the cold, hard ground, the ritual murmur of the rosary vibrating in low, chanting waves. Imagine those hundred men, our men, I said to my mother in the scullery, only last night, denying their bodies food for as long as it took to be treated as prisoners of war. The hunger strike is a violent, often final, thing, but I kept that thought to myself. The workers came out in such force for the hunger strikers, today. So I wasn't too surprised that Mary and her friends wanted to parade in their own way their budding republicanism.

When she finally looked over to acknowledge me, she nodded a smile of reassurance; *these men need my support just as much as yours*, her ardent expression had communicated. She was now far beyond being told how Mountjoy was no place for a girl her age, at any time, never mind now, in the moments and hours before a huge public outcry crushed onto the streets of Dublin. Already, the military were struggling to hold back men and women who were being carried along by the weight of others behind them. Just as Mary turned back to her work, Captain Brennan ushered me back to my task of organizing more of the cordons; a fierce urgency had gripped the air. A howl of a gale tore round us as more workers filed into the street in their hundreds, then thousands. So strange to realize that people trickled, then poured out of their work this afternoon; all those abandoned trains, halted trams, closed shops, deserted factory floors. Agitated voices soon drowned out the keening women and their rosary prayers. Every now and then a burst of ballad and hymn song could be heard in small pockets of the heaving mass of supporters.

C na mB members were scattered throughout the entire area; order and safety were paramount to us. It had become clear that the police and troops were overwhelmed. Some soldiers just seemed to stand still, hiding behind their fixed bayonets, their eyes darting here and there; fractious scuffles daring them to use their weapons. One or two tanks rumbled their heavy presence but the enormous crowd simply ignored them. In the end, the military left most of the crowd control to us and our safety barricades. The trouble, they could see, had been minimized; not so barbaric, after all, their relieved faces said.

We made passages for relatives who were allowed into the prison grounds. We cleared a space for a good number of doctors who waited at the main entrance should they be needed. And whenever the weakest of the prisoners were carried out on stretchers some of our members insisted on accompanying them in ambulances to the hospitals; we had to keep a record of who was going where so that we could let their families know.

When C na mB reinforcements arrived in the evening, Captain Brennan sent my unit home. I found Mary at her safety cordon and she was told to go with me. She linked her arm through mine for the long walk home. I listened as she described in detail an incident she'd heard about from the demonstrators. Some grief-stricken women broke through the outer iron gates demanding to see the prisoners. The men inside, Mary said, were their husbands and sons and the women were desperately worried. She said it was easy for them to get past the inner gate post and on into the prison buildings. A woman told her later that the warders couldn't cope and there were rumours of some prisoners smashing furniture and breaking through cell walls.

It was dark by the end of her story and I was exhausted. The bitter wind had died down but the evening had grown cold.

'Do you think we'll win this war when the hunger strike is over, Dervla?' She squeezed my arm closer to her young body and waited for my response. We had been walking along the quiet quays towards the lower end of the Liffey when she asked this huge question which had no coherent answer.

'Let's pray these men will be granted their rights before we talk about winning the war.' It was all I could say to her.

So, Dublin has downed tools and gathered itself into a general strike. The authorities will not be able to cope with the idle defiance of their second city.

I need to rest in case tomorrow is another long day. It feels too self-indulgent to mark my birthday this evening. Besides, twenty seven is hardly a milestone worth bothering about.

Gelignite Baby, Thursday, 6th May 1920

Captain Brennan wanted 'an older girl' from Central Branch, someone without her own children. The Commandant of the army's First Battalion had told the Captain whoever she selected was to meet two women operatives off one of the friendly trading ships at North Wall. His order made it clear that the operatives were to be brought out of the docklands, on foot, towards the city centre, to a safe house on Gloucester Street. In relative comfort and privacy, the women would be able to unwind the tightly bound fuse from their arms and remove the rectangular parcels of gelignite from their torsos.

A small room at the back of the safe house is frequently used by C na mB for baby clubs where mothers and grandmothers have meetings and plan the logistics of whatever they might be transporting round the city. Their prams play a vital role. My own mother told me the women prefer when their babies cry as the soldiers aren't inclined to pay them too much attention, ushering them on along the street so they don't have to listen to the wailing. The stark absence of the men, my mother said, means the prams are often the only tactic deployed by many of the women.

The two women were to rest upstairs before being escorted by another C na mB member to the boat train at Westland Row which would take them to Kingstown where they would board the next mail steamer back to England. The fuse and the sticks of gelignite I was to hide carefully in a pram, then leave the house with a designated mother and her baby boy, and walk the rest of the way into the city. Our destination was above Moreland Cabinetmakers on Abbey Street.

Everything went according to plan. Until after three or four minutes of walking on Talbot Street, towards the city, along a terrace of various shops occupying the ground level of red brick dwellings, when we saw an armoured car reversing slowly, and horribly, in our direction. Large, mud-stained wheels rumbling like subdued thunder on the surface of the road. The military, probably that new Black and Tan crowd, about to raid a nearby house, or shop. They were too far down the street if the Republican Outfitters at no. 94 was their target. No matter who the Tans were after it would be rough and noisy, a confusion we could take advantage of by walking straight through it; there was no other road to take, anyway. Or it could go another way; we might be a frivolous distraction for them, especially if they had drink

151

taken. I had to think quickly. I suddenly felt enormously responsible for the young mother and her baby boy. He had started to whimper slightly in his drowsy sleep. I didn't even know their names.

It so happened there was a small flower stall jutting out onto the footpath where we had stopped in our tracks near the military patrol. The old man at the stall had about four bunches of purple freesias left to sell. A picture of Edmund arranging the same flowers for Nellie Franny as she lay weakening in her bed pressed into the back of my mind. The old man's eyes took in the scene of us women standing there with the pram, the armoured car getting closer. The neighbouring shops were quietly closing their doors tight, a moving track of clicking and shutting I didn't at first notice. I looked directly at the stall owner, the shape of a frantic appeal on my lips, when he dipped behind some empty flower buckets and grabbed a thick wedge of brown paper. The young mother, a slight girl of about twenty, moved closer to me and grabbed the side of the pram handles, as though she might be getting ready to climb in beside her infant son.

When the old man handed me the remaining freesias, hastily wrapped and bound, I started to say I had no money to pay him. It then occurred to me that he may have been trying to get rid of us so that he wouldn't bring any unwanted attention upon himself. 'They'll want to search the flowers before thinking of the baby's pram,' he said. He pointed his head towards a group of soldiers who were by this stage on foot and banging on a closed door about three shops from the flower stall. The armoured vehicle had stopped its backward crawl. 'Just walk right past them, and remember to let them see the flowers.' The old man pressed his palm at my elbow, a gentle push forward. Before I could utter a word to him he turned quickly away from us and immersed himself in the casual stacking away of his flowerless buckets, the end of a busy afternoon's selling on his humble outdoor flower stall, no raid to worry about, no furtive vanishing required.

And so that's what we did. I remained on the left side of the pram and gathered an auntly aura around myself in the way I assisted my young 'niece' in steering her pram. I cradled the purple flowers dramatically across my chest with my left arm. I could feel the girl shaking into my other arm as we pushed in unison. The baby had settled into a dreamy slumber. Snugly encased as he was in his soft, butter-coloured woollen blanket, a second one, thinner, made of cotton, moulded over the tightly coiled fuse and greaseproof-papered explosives beneath. 'Act as if we have the street to ourselves,' I whispered to the mother from the corner of my mouth.

Take all your emotion out of the next few seconds, I told myself, as we walked purposely past the broken down door the Tans were by now filing themselves through like reckless burglars. Their mismatched uniforms adding a new layer of terror. Don't look inside the hallway, don't gaze through the windows, don't strain to listen to the voices of the shopkeeper's family who no doubt live in the upstairs rooms. Will they plead for the non-destruction of their furniture, the goods in their shop, their lives? Think about this baby, I ordered myself.

The soldiers, it seemed to us, had been oblivious to us passing by. We had reached the corner of Talbot Place. We could either take a left towards Beresford Place, or continue in the direction of O'Connell Street. I felt the young mother's grip loosen slightly on my arm. But our relief was shattered as we stepped towards our original destination of the city centre.

'You two lovely ladies are in a bit of a hurry, aren't you?' A familiar enough accent; Scottish, Glaswegian, perhaps, biting at our heels, getting closer.

We stopped, rigid, and waited. My mind snatched a line of talk from the air which might appease the voice. I turned my head to greet his boyish smile with one of my own. A matronly smile which lacked the grain of flirtation, or anxiety, he may have been expecting. 'And indeed we might be, sir. We need to get to my sister's bedside, she's very weak with her heart. My young niece here is terribly worried about her mother. We think the sight of the grandchild and these fresh blooms might uplift her spirits and give her strength.'

Taking slow strides, he circled us, eventually stopping in front of me. He was no more than twenty one. The barrel of his rifle pointed lazily towards the hood of the baby's pram. His expression altered a little towards something resembling remembered authority; in deference to me, the older woman in front of him, or in retaliation, I couldn't tell in that moment. I felt the tremble of the girl's nerves begin to get the better of her beside me.

'And where would the sick lady be residing?'

'Down beyond the quays, up at Manor Street. So you'll see we have a distance yet to walk.'

'Do you mind holding out the flowers so I can take a closer look at them, madam,' he asked. A note of formality tinged his request.

'Not at all, but please be careful if you touch them, the freesia is a delicate enough flower.'

The angle of the rifle's barrel fell slowly towards the ground as he palmed the length and circumference of the brown paper wrapping with one hand. He rubbed his index finger along the opening ridge of the paper and brought the flowers downwards in order to look inside the package. He then tipped the bundle back in my direction. I didn't move a muscle as I watched him remove his cap and bend his head to look carefully into the pram. 'Do you have anything else for your poorly sister?' He raised his head slightly from the pram and looked at me, waiting for an answer.

The other soldiers had become nosier in their demands for names, munitions, hidden stockpiles of whatever might or might not be on the premises. A vague somewhere else type of noise I could hear intermittently through the pounding of my own heart which seemed to be thrashing the bloodied substance of itself against my rib cage, desperate to hurl itself out of my body.

Just as my eyes shifted from his, an involuntary move, barely perceptible, one of the young mother's legs creased at the knee and a low keening sob jumped from her mouth. I grabbed her by the waist and elbow to stop her entire body from crumpling on to the road, the freesias slipping from my hand. I glared at the young soldier and dared to admonish him as though he were half his age. 'Your mention of her sick mother has upset her something terrible. We really need to be getting on, sir.'

The baby had started to emerge from his deep sleep, stretching his milky arms and tiny determined fists. The loud crack and spark of a single gunshot being fired inside the shop was the trigger for his instant scream of fright. His eyes, brimming with terror, wide open to the awful intrusion. By now, the soldier had straightened himself from the pram, the intensified raid a renewed source of distraction.

'Okay, Madam, I think we're finished here, anyway. I hope your mum gets better, miss.'

And he was gone from our side.

Without turning to witness what we knew would torment us later - should we have tried to distract the Tans from raiding that shop? could we have appealed to them to at least let the family out into the street? - we walked quickly along the remaining length of Talbot Street, towards the mass of people, the rush and ramble of our city, and away from a nameless, terrorized family. We made sure to take a few cautionary diversions before heading for Moreland's on Abbey Street. I had left the flowers on the footpath, where they fell, on the corner of Talbot Place, an abandoned and beautiful memorial to a random suffering we did nothing to stop.

A Home to Rule, Thursday, 17th June 1920

Nuala and I had to change our plans to stroll up to the Bohemian in Phibsborough today. We'd been looking forward to seeing which afternoon picture was showing as we hadn't been back since *Willy Reilly and his Colleen Bawn* was on. Watching that picture had taken me straight back to Limehouse in London when Nellie Franny told me about her Protestant sweetheart. Nuala and I were also desperate to have a bit of normality for a couple of hours.

Near Parnell Square we spotted Colm, an old friend of Seamus's, walking deliberately towards us in the busy street. I remember when Colm used to visit our house the odd evening before the Tans arrived from England. When we were close enough, Colm gestured a polite good afternoon and as he did so pressed a folded envelope into my hand. Nuala told me to forget our walk to the picture theatre and go straight home and read whatever was inside the envelope, in private.

Dear Dervla,

I am ashamed that me or John haven't come to see how you've been since the military raided the house. We got your message but it was too risky to reply. John says it couldn't be helped but I know he feels responsible. There are plenty gaining favours from the Castle giving names of lads in the I.R.A.. Sometimes we don't know who to trust.

But the Big Fella is a smart and fair man. He has John working as an Intelligence Officer with others from the Second and Third Battalions. The men in Mick's Squad are paid full-time wages. Sure they don't know themselves.

When I think of what the Tans are doing up and down the country, the intimidations and shootings and the burning of people's properties. I have to believe that it'll end one day and the country will be our own again.

And I know you believe the same, Dervla. Remember all the literature you used to show me? It was you who taught me about nationalism. It made more sense to me as I got older. You said that securing home rule is one thing, but it isn't everything. That it is like owning your own house, but being told by another how to live in it. That idea has stayed with me, Dervla, it has inspired me. I will always be grateful for such learning. Listen to me going on.

John sends his love. This war weighs heavily on him at times. I don't think he'll ever forgive himself for not speaking up when Rory received his order to leave Jacob's. He blames himself for his death, Dervla. For not protecting his friend. And for ruining that time in your life because of it. He worries terribly about you but he's glad you're back.

Destroy this letter. We'll visit as soon as we can.

Your loving brother, Seamus

I reread Seamus's letter this evening before destroying it, as he asked. All traces have now been burnt down into ashes, no evidence of his contact. Except of course here, in my diary. I know my precious diary is safe for a little longer. Soon, I will have no need for it.

I am now sitting in front of the warm fire thinking about John's long suffering over Rory. If only we'd had more time together last year; we talked about me, but not a word about Rory. And I barely saw him or Seamus when they brought poor injured Pat to the house in February. I know I've had dark moments when I've stood still and imagined shards of John's guilt cutting into his heart; now I know he must have, at times, felt these cuts. Wasn't this darkness one of the reasons I took myself off to London? The place I met Edmund.

And it would appear I've run from him too. Without giving him a proper chance to change his whole life for a new one with me. Seamus's letter has made me want to find out if the door to that life is still open. I need to write to Edmund again, to ask him to visit me, like we'd planned. Seeing him face to face, in Dublin, is the only way I can explain again why I had to leave him, this time with the full truth of my secret actions, all of them. I'll have to warn him that his recent letters to me may be with the censors, or even destroyed. Our contact has become misaligned, the chaos of our new war with England has thrown our correspondence asunder. I've also let that happen. Like I did with John's guilt.

Daylight Posters, Saturday, 10th July 1920

Well, if today's activities awaken any small thing in the hearts of a few more Dubliners, especially the ones that need an extra jolt, I'll be happy enough.

Pasting as many posters and bulletins as you can manage onto as many lamp posts and walls that'll take them, as fast as you can, is bloody hard work. What's harder is spotting the armed patrols and their spies before they see the detail of what it is you're doing; a young woman reaching up and jabbing and rubbing the surface of a random post, on a random street.

Nuala and I used friendly, tactical diversions to carry out our work. We flitted along the length of Henry Street before heading up round Mary Street and beyond. Being female came in handy, of course. We worked fast and were each other's eyes. We moved as one interchangeable unit with two parts; while one did the job of demure-eyed lookout, the other made sure the bulletins were prominently displayed. Of course scores of passers-by simply ignored us, but just as many more made sure to signal their allegiance by doing what they could to shield us from any unwanted attention.

Central Branch had briefed us on Propaganda and Publicity's clear instructions that we were to work in pairs, to mobilize throughout the city centre, and to target as many surfaces as possible. A bit of a reminder of the barbaric prison conditions, here and across the water, or the atrocities being committed all over the country, the captain had said, was exactly what many in Dublin needed to have stuck in front of them. Broad daylight crowds and busy streets were our natural armour. Night curfews and pitch darkness bring their own risks to the women.

If only Nellie Franny had been with me and Nuala, today. I don't think she did any poster work in London but she used to weave in and out of London-Irish public meetings, handing out bulletins, making new contacts. Now, we're carrying on with that work here, in Dublin. Except of course, God rest her soul, Nellie Franny is no longer by my side.

A letter from Edmund, Wednesday, 21st July 1920

My dearest Dervla,

I can't tell you what it meant to receive your letter. I'm ashamed to say my letters weren't intercepted, I simply stopped writing to you. I thought that if I tried to forget you, like Father kept suggesting, you'd get tired of waiting and eventually meet someone else. Someone like Rory. The name you called out once or twice while in the fevered grip of the influenza virus. I told myself that I simply couldn't compete with him. I knew he was someone you lost in the Rising - it was written on your face whenever you spoke of the losses. Your eyes would cloud over and just for a moment a great sadness would take you away from me. Of course, I should have asked who you were thinking about, but it felt like too much of an intrusion into your private life. There it is, the coward in me, yet again. Just not brave enough.

I'm afraid to say I began to feel terribly sorry for myself.

I became a bit of a recluse. Father let me stew in it and pretended everything was in order. But then Helena opened my eyes. When I didn't respond to Charlie's Spring invitations to dinner or drinks, Helena came to the house, alone, and demanded to know why I was hiding myself away. I think she knew the truth of it all along. I told her about you and I planning a life together in Ireland. And about what turned out to be my reluctance to actually leave with you last year. She wasn't surprised, she said the hold my father had over me was sometimes palpable. Dervla, I know now how thoughtless it was of me to introduce you to him during the Peace holiday. That day must have been hellish for you. I'm afraid my father is the kind of person who does not share your views on the Irish question. But I do, you know I do. And I am nothing like my father.

I found myself also confiding in Helena about my self-loathing about getting out of fighting in the war, and my feelings of shame about Charlie. She went very quiet and then told me that what Charlie himself is too proud to tell me is that every day he is tormented by the enormous fatalities of the war, the sheer loss of life overwhelms him. He tortures himself by going over every decision, every order, every tactical approach, like a man obsessed. And every night he is plagued by the most horrific nightmares. It seems he is a broken man, Dervla. There is so much as an officer that he cannot come to terms with. Helena said he is filled with a monstrous sense of guilt. She is a strong woman and I know she will help him through it.

She begged me to overcome my demons before it was too late, to consider the notion that perhaps it was fate that you and I were placed in Poplar on that same mournful day. That the gods conspired it that way so we could somehow

save each other from our own torments. Not sacrifice each
other, as I was allowing myself to do.

And then I got your letter. I felt like I'd been given a
blessed chance to redeem myself, to ask you to forgive my
pathetic behaviour, and to begin that new life of serving
Ireland we'd planned. I've never stopped loving you,
Dervla. You're right, we do have so much to talk about.
And we will. I finally told Father I am leaving for Ireland
early in October. I have already started making the
necessary arrangements. This is my promise to you, my love.
Wait for me.

Yours, Edmund

So there it is, the second chance I've been holding
out for. I'm not too sure what I should be feeling.
It's an honest letter, I'll give Edmund that, alright.
I don't think he will ever be more ready than now
to break away from his life and family to be with
me; this will be his ultimate sacrifice. I must
prepare myself to bear my soul in return. By the
time he arrives there will be more secrets about
me he will need to hear. I will seem altered to him;
will he recognize me? I pray that our love will
survive the darkness ahead.

A Collins Girl, Friday, 13th August 1920

I should have walked out of the club and gone
with the messenger boy to Capel Street. Those
biscuit tins, unstacked from the trolley, cradled in
his young arms, would have appeared heavy.
Biscuit tins aren't supposed to look heavy.
Perhaps he had a handcart out back with other

provisions already neatly loaded; an ordinary errand delivering across the city to a sister club. I'll never know if he arrived safely.

It's late now, after 1.00am, and I can't sleep. Nuala asked me only yesterday would I stand in for her at the private club where she does the odd shift, as she wanted to go out to Blackrock for tea with her Niall. I knew the United Services Club paid their kitchen hands a few shillings more than the hotels so I told her I'd do it, no problem.

What a beautiful but imposing building facing itself grandly onto St. Stephen's Green. Tonight it was full of British officers. As I found my way to the kitchen below stairs, I caught a glimpse of them sitting in one of the dining rooms on the ground floor. The large room sparkled with British maleness. An incongruous sight, when you think about it. The elite of the British military sitting politely in the chandeliered light, the best of linen lying across their uniformed laps, crystal glasses full of expensive wine in their hands, gleaming silver cutlery waiting to be held. Less of a guardedness about some of them, a thing I couldn't quite put my finger on in that brief glimpse.

I was glad to report to the head cook and slip into the clamour and heat of the kitchen, its close smells of gamey joints and rich sauces owning the hot air. All you'll be doing is helping with mountains of vegetables, Nuala had said. And that's exactly what the job was - cleaning, peeling, shredding, dicing, and chopping vegetables - and I can tell you I've never seen so many of the things in my whole life; hundreds of potatoes, carrots, onions, turnips. I got stuck in and worked quickly. Everyone in the kitchen was busy with concentration, listening and shouting as their tasks dictated. Most seemed to be Dubliners, and most were friendly. A permitted toilet break was my chance to take in the splendour of the building and it was on my way back down to the kitchen when I saw her standing, very still, outside a slightly open door, along a quiet corridor, away from and to the left of the sweeping staircase.

It must be that Collins girl, Molly O'Reilly, I thought, the one who organizes safe houses. Nuala had said Molly would probably be in tonight but that she's leaving the club soon to work in the Bonne Bouche tearooms round the corner on Dawson Street. There are Collins girls, and boys, working undercover all over the city. They stand behind shop counters, check coats in hotel cloakrooms, serve food in restaurants, and file and type letters in Dublin Castle. All sorts of information hovering within earshot, or placed right in front of their eyes. Some of the girls are still in C na mB but they generally keep themselves to themselves, often preferring to work alone, the way Mick Collins seems to like it. But I wonder can any of us fully trust each other any more? Especially since all the suppressions last year. Being less visible during a war isn't always a good thing in such a small, furtive city.

It was a foolish risk, I know, but I told myself if she was who I suspected she was I had a duty to offer her assistance, however small. The reddish hair, her youth, the casual readiness into which she might engage or disappear on the spot – these small observations convinced me I was right. When I saw her swiftly enter the room I made my move along the corridor.

She hadn't closed the door from the inside; that would indicate far too much intent. But she didn't hear me push quietly into the room - the Gentlemen's Room, the polished door sign told me - seconds after her. I expected the room to be all wood panelling and heavy furniture, but it was much more informal, untidy in places, with hats and summer overcoats and various trunks arranged hurriedly on stands and along the length of one dark wall. Half smoked cigarettes stubbed out in saucers and the fiery aroma of whiskey remnants in the bottom of crystal tumblers occupied one or two glass-topped tables. Had the gentlemen and army officers taken the liberty of pouring their own drinks, tired of waiting for a lowly clerk who had decided they could uncoat and serve themselves?

And then I saw what held her attention.

The Sam Browns were hanging from a set of brass pegs unadorned with outdoor garments. They were suspended by their leather straps and their pearl handles made them look like special theatre props, waiting in their designated spaces, not yet required by the main players; the unguarded look I had noticed when passing the dining room on my way to the kitchen to report for work.

Her natural instinct obviously told her a pair of

eyes were on her because in that moment she turned fully to greet me, a radiant smile on her face and ten different scenarios poised on her lips. 'Ah, I see the manager got my message, have you been sent to help me clear up this mess?' A wide sweep of her arm took in the cigarette ends and tumblers while her other hand smoothed down her uniform apron.

I guessed her time was rigidly measured.

'Yes, I'm here to help you in any way I can.' I let her see my eyes settle on the hanging revolvers. 'My name is Dervla and I'm covering in the kitchen for a close friend who I work with at number 25.' The voice in my head prayed she would catch my C na mB reference, the same voice which also told me to say no more to this young girl. I knew she had a split second to make her judgement about me. Her blue eyes blazed alertness. She held her smile while she regarded me, inclining her head slightly to the right. Did she believe me? Could she trust a sudden stranger?

'I'm Molly and the storeroom beside the kitchen has exactly what I need to do my work here,' she said, moving closer to the brass pegs.

Three of the tables Molly was charged with looking after were military officers, each one of them having ordered three courses. She explained they would be expecting their main meals of venison, pork, or duck, in about ten minutes. Waiting on tables and serving food is a perfect cover, she said, especially while trying to gather useful intelligence in the amiable hours after dessert, but a waitress not stationed at the service hatch at the right time would seem strange to staff and patrons.

Molly needed me to work fast. Not being on familiar terms with the kitchen staff was a minor disadvantage so I had to get straight back to preparing my vegetables without arousing suspicion. Or give the appearance of doing so. I chopped rapidly through bunched carrots while counting inside my head two full minutes. The club had other non-military diners to cater for so the kitchen was continually busy with various courses. Thank God for it as this ensured a mild chaos throughout the order of service. Molly had told me precisely where in the storeroom to find three large empty Jacobs biscuit tins, plus a bundle of tea-cloths, none of which would be missed by anybody during my shift. Afterwards, it wouldn't matter; we'd be long gone.

She had also told me exactly what to say to the messenger boy, another friend, who was usually to be found near the main reception desk. This I did first. I saw him immediately. He had years yet to fill his work uniform. He listened intently and when I stopped talking he moved away from me, nodding like he'd been in this situation many times. Which, of course, one way or another, he had.

Molly had locked herself into the Gentlemen's Room with a key she had copied a week ago. She had planned on getting the kitchen items herself but my decision to follow her saved her five precious minutes. A stroke of good fortune she had said I was, as she ushered me out the door.

As arranged, the messenger boy was wheeling an almost empty trolley slowly along the Gentlemen's Room corridor as I went about my own business of carrying the biscuit tins and tea-cloths. He had an old, jangly trolley, perfect for members' discarded tea cups and plates, used glasses and cutlery. A subdued but distinctive sound-signal for Molly to unlock the door from the inside. I passed by the young boy and walked into the room. I'd been involved in enough actions to know that focusing on the plan was paramount to success. To anybody who cared to glance beyond the staircase to their left, they would see a perfectly normal scene: messenger boy; trolley; kitchen girl; sundry items.

Molly and I had the revolvers wrapped in the tea-cloths and placed inside the Jacobs biscuit tins by the sound of the trolley's second signal. I opened the door and the boy trundled inside. At that point our work became even more deliberate and efficient. Soon the trolley was full with crystal tumblers, littered trays of used china, discarded tobacco, and spools of fallen ash, as well as the large biscuit tins, no longer empty. Before I had time to say goodbye to either of them they were already on their way to their next task: the boy, somehow, to take the hidden revolvers to Dinny O'Callaghan's leather shop on Capel Street, and Molly, with one minute to spare, to retrieve the officers' piping hot main meals from the service hatch and serve them as if she'd been in obedient attendance since the first course.

I might have caught the pleasant strains of a string quartet floating on the air from one of the other private rooms as I dashed below stairs to resume my work. I can't be sure, I may have imagined the idea of music. The rest of the evening raced by as the kitchen received fresh orders of everything. I remained beside my heap of vegetables and recounted back to myself every detail of our mission, as I'm doing now.

I wonder if I will ever work with Molly O'Reilly, or the young messenger, again. I can't wait to tell Nuala what she missed last night.

Escalation, Tuesday, 31st August 1920

There have been terrible murders throughout the country by the Black and Tans. And now there is this other crowd in Dublin, the Auxiliaries, apparently more brutal. Whatever, they all amount to the same murderous thing: paramilitaries, ex-soldiers and officers with killing in their hearts and cheap alcohol in their blood. Jesus Christ, why are they in our country? Do you not have it in your divine power to drive them away from our own streets and fields?

And I am distraught as there is still no news from Seamus or John. Nothing since Seamus's letter. Where are they? May God keep them both safe from those Tan bastards. I can only think my brothers are deliberately staying well away from our house in order to protect us.

I've been at home with Mary and Mam for a lot of the day. It's been a quiet day in this city. Too quiet.

I haven't seen Nuala properly in a while. When I told her about Edmund's plans to come to Ireland, she said she was delighted at the prospect of finally meeting him. So I could do with one of our chats, just to shake out my nerves a little. Apart from the practical challenges of Edmund coming here I can't help feeling a tiny bit overwhelmed at the thought of our reunion. I'll see if I can prise Nuala away from Niall for an evening or two.

Hunger Strike, Friday, 3rd September 1920

Terence MacSwiney, the Lord Mayor of Cork, and other hunger strikers, are dying in Brixton Prison. To think, that could easily be one of my own brothers wasting away in God only knows what kind of putrid conditions. Or Rory, if he was still alive, today. Only to die on me all over again. Prayers are being said for all of them in churches across the land. St Bride's, among other clubs in England, are no doubt praying for Mr MacSwiney as he continues his hunger campaign over there.

I might be imagining things but I think I'm being followed. A thin shadow of a man lurking and dipping in and out of my sight. Another shadow among many which flit in every place in Dublin. It wouldn't surprise me if Mr Churchfield, even at this stage, is trying to sabotage Edmund's journey by hiring some drip of an underling to spy on me. To rake up the dirt he's convinced anchors me to the nefarious city his son is being pulled towards.

North King Street Ambush, Monday, 20th September 1920

There was an ambush outside the bakery on North King Street today. Two or three soldiers were shot. I heard that a young I.R.A. man was captured at the scene. There were more with him, but the word is they ran away.

Seamus finally came to see us only yesterday. He tried to persuade us to leave the house and stay with Aunty Kathleen for a few weeks because it isn't safe for people who live so close to Kilmainham prison. He put on a brave face of brotherly authority but I knew he was hiding something from me. And that story about living near the prison seemed unlikely; Kathleen's house is not much further from it than ours. Is it the same if you live on the doorstep of Mountjoy and the other prisons? But I pushed my suspicious thoughts away as I wanted to relish every moment with my brother. I hadn't seen him for so long and there was so much to tell each other. And then, without saying goodbye, Seamus was gone before dawn.

Now, there is chaos in the streets; soldiers are searching everywhere for the others involved in the bakery ambush.

Mam has just handed me a short letter from John. Seamus gave it to her late last night. She told me to burn it when I finished reading it. Just as I did with Seamus's last letter, when I copy it into this diary, I'll destroy it.

Dear Dervla

I need to explain to you what I can about the night Rory was shot. Being on active service in a war demands the most difficult of decisions. Hard decisions, hard orders, which are loaded with the weight of violence you are not permitted to flinch from. I have been handed my fair share of them. Not questioning the order to send Rory out alone that night was one of the worst I have to live with. I never ever wanted you to find yourself in such a torturous position. But I know now it was a mistake to be so presumptuous. You are your own person, and I am proud of you.

Yours, John

John, wherever you are tonight, stay safe for me.

Balbriggan Burns, Tuesday, 21st September

I've just come from a C na mB meeting after evening mass in the Pro Cathedral. Captain Brennan reported extensive raids and looting last night in Balbriggan, a village about thirty miles north of the city. It's a place I've never been to but just like Dublin its streets are full of ordinary, decent families. It's now almost certain there were at least two cold-blooded murders committed by the military in the town. As if that wasn't awful enough, others were beaten and homes and businesses pulverized. Up and down our beloved country this exact same thing has been happening.

And then another verified report from one of the younger girls, Máire. She described a brutal reprisals attack on five of our women in Galway. The Black and Tans shaved the women's heads in front of an elderly couple and their grandchildren. The women had been using a friendly farmer's barn for a secret meeting when a Crossley Tender screeched to a halt outside, nearly crashing into the only door. The women had no means of escape and had to endure the cruel spectacle of each other's forced humiliation.

Máire said each woman was ordered to kneel down and, while two or three Tans restrained her by the arms and shoulders, another one stood behind her and pulled chunks of her hair violently against his blade. They took it in turns to violate each woman in this way. Apparently one of the Tans complained that the physical resistance and thrashing exhausted him, put him off his concentration. The rough hacking and wrenching of blade and hair tore into the women's scalps and bloodied their faces and necks.

Máire told us why the Black and Tans attacked our Galway women. A terrified woman had given evidence in court against the I.R.A. who subsequently took it upon themselves to punish her with a republican scalping.

I feel immense sorrow for the Balbriggan people, but what the Tans did to those women in Galway is burning and twisting into my conscience. Because also within our own network of I.R.A. boys and their Battalions the same orders are being followed in other dark corners; women who ignore the boycott on having contact with the military, or giving evidence like the woman Máire mentioned, having their hair ripped from their heads.

My own brothers are based in and around Dublin and they would be appalled at such degrading I.R.A. reprisals in the countryside. Wouldn't they?

A Day of Mourning, Monday, 25th October 1920

A general holiday has been called today throughout Ireland. Terence MacSwiney is dead.

His emaciated body will be brought to his people down in Cork. There are great crowds out here in Dublin to mourn him. Fear and anger permeate the fabric of all things. The world it seems is outraged; our plight is illuminated.

No word yet from Edmund. How stupid of me to believe he would actually go ahead and defy his father. I wonder what the two of them thought when the voice on their wireless told them of Terence MacSwiney's death after over seventy days of hunger strike. Were they sitting in the drawing room when the news was broadcast? Did Edmund appease his father by having little or no opinion on the matter?

I must press my energies into looking out for young Mary and my mother. Perhaps there was something to what Seamus said a few weeks back about us staying with Kathleen for a while. Women minding women while they protect men. Men and boys running, running, still running. When will all this disappearance stop?

Shadows, Wednesday, 27th October 1920

I think I got a good look at the snake who has been following me. It wasn't my imagination, after all. A tall scrape of a man stretched into his oily skin of dark wool, flitting in and out of my sight, as I walked home slowly this afternoon. He wore a pristine, stiff white collar which seemed stitched into his spindly neck. Nothing at all Irish about his look, or gait. I didn't let on I'd seen him.

I need to be certain this is the shadowy figure who has been watching me since last month. Since the ambush, and God knows all the other things that have been turning my city inside out, I just can't assume anything. He could be some class of a government worker, for all I know. I don't need to remind myself of the very real possibility that the military are constantly waiting for me to lead them to the brothers I never see. At this time, in this city, everyone is fair game to Dublin Castle.

But if he's not from the Castle, what then does this scrawny character, who looks like he strolled out of the pages of Edgar Allan Poe, want from me? Something about his pale, wiry face leaches the work of Mr Churchfield. Would Edmund's father go to such elaborately ridiculous lengths to keep his precious son away from me? He must still be furious at my dismissal of his insidious letter. My not responding to - not the merest acknowledgement of - his insulting litany of requests must have infuriated him, grated at his superior English pride. A man demented by the insubordination of an Irish girl whom his son insisted on loving. He couldn't find a way to separate us in London, so now it would appear he is spying on me in my own city.

Yes, he probably thinks he has all the ammunition he needs in the very fact of my Irishness. What on earth does he think he can achieve? The tiniest scrap of evidence, something poisoned by his hand, in order to finally feel vindicated. *Look, my dear Edmund, it's what I've been trying to tell you all this time, that girl is no good for you, it's pure folly to concoct a future with her type.* The father's annihilation of the son's true, but unfortunate, love for the little seamstress who forgets that she is also a skivvy. The whole business of our love for each other is a nasty and inconvenient nuisance to Mr Churchfield, an ill-fated alliance which to him is not only completely unacceptable, it is utterly inconceivable.

But who am I fooling here? How is Mr Churchfield's deviousness, such as it is, any worse than my own? There are facets and crevices to Edmund's treasured Dervla he still has no idea of. To put it starkly, she is a liar. She has been lying to him since the moment she agreed to place those revolvers in the lining of her overcoat. See, there it is, a cold appraisal of myself. Written in my own hand. Un-take-back-able.

And I remind myself this evening, there is no alliance, no relationship, any more, is there? Not while I'm here and he's there. He is yet to step off the mail boat in Kingstown; he promised to get here in early October. October is nearly over. I have so much I need to tell him. And yet, I'm still trying to convince myself that we will be reunited soon. Soon. Does that word ever have a definitive date? The war kept us together. Its reality cocooned us in London. The ghost of Edmund's so-called exemption may, despite Helena's warnings, haunt him until it consumes him. And this war, my own country's war, is pulling us apart, fibre by fibre. A coward and a fool is what I am to dare imagine a life of bliss here, in Ireland. Anyway, it seems Edmund will never betray his father's wishes. He no longer needs to use words of defiance to ask his permission; I can hear the bladed silence between them from here - solid and unmoving - on the forbidden subject of dearest Dervla.

Anonymous, Friday, 29th October 1920

This unsigned note, addressed to me, was shoved under our front door early this morning:

> Your family are seen as enemies to the Crown. Sever all contact with E.C. The military have connected your brother to the ambush on Monk's bakery. It is a matter of time with your other brother. The first raid was a friendly warning. Don't expect your brothers or anyone else to be around to protect you from the second raid.

Who on earth wrote this note? The military surely wouldn't send me such a clear warning themselves, and I don't really know any Castle workers who'd have access to this kind of information. Unless Niall is more of a friend of ours than I took him for. But I haven't seen him, or Nuala, not properly, for ages. So, is it a note of rough intimidation, or a friendly warning?

Now, the cold thought that Edmund himself has betrayed me in some horrendous way is in my head. Buying promised time until this day? All those stories I shared with him about my brothers and the Volunteers. But his father is not a military man. Unless, of course, he is and the stark fact of it has been staring me in the face since the day I met his son. Dear Lord, how powerful a man is he? I just thought he wanted us separated. *The first raid was a friendly warning.* The polite officer. Now, there is to be a second raid. The Black and Tans. Or those Auxiliaries. But when?

After dinner, I will calmly tell Mam that I need her to pack a few things and take Mary on the first tram on Sunday morning into the city. They will go to mass in the Pro Cathedral before taking another tram towards the brewery, to Aunty Kathleen's house. There they will stay for three or four days until I can come for them. I will make it clear to my mother, without explaining the specifics of why, that she must not be alarmed, and that she must trust me. And I know she will.

Telegram, Saturday, 30th October 1920

A telegram from the Shelbourne Hotel arrived early this morning. It has been folded in my pocket all day. It tells me that Edmund has arrived in Dublin. At last, after all this time, he is finally here. He is staying in the Shelbourne Hotel. That is nice for him. The telegram also tells me he will wait at the hotel for me for as long as it takes and that he will explain his lateness in person. I wonder if he has any other explaining to do. Perhaps he's discovered how far his father is willing to go to keep us apart. Well, my love, you *will* have to wait. I may never get to join you in the Shelbourne Hotel.

I need to be close enough to this house today so that I can protect my mother and sister before they leave in the morning. I cannot ignore the warning note about another raid. It now seems imminent that Kevin Barry, the young student who was arrested last month, will hang unless he gives up the other names of those involved in the bakery ambush. I've already promised Central Branch I'd help with the prison dinners at Mountjoy tomorrow. The Barry family will be there too.

So, my reunion with Edmund, all that we have to share with each other, is no longer my priority.

This Dread Love
Monday, 1st November 1920

The last of this waiting is almost upon me.

Many entries for the last days of my diary are almost indecipherable, even to me: rubbed over pencil marks, words written on top of others, stunted sentences running diagonally across two of the pages, unfinished shorthand notes, random phrases coded in Irish. I move the diary away from me to one side of the wooden table. I need to recollect key moments of the past couple of days, particularly the last twenty four hours, those details unrecorded by my hand. There hasn't been the time.

So, now, a final entry, you could say. Unwritten. Invisible.

It seems vitally important that I concentrate my mind; I may want to retell my story from memory, one day, in a future I now find strange to imagine.

As I stand at the window, watching and waiting, I notice how the day outside has slipped into a bitterly cold afternoon. The light is steel grey and parched. I pull the felt collar of my coat closer to my neck and take a long, deep breath. I know the recall of my clandestine meeting with John last night must be rapid. Unless my ears are deceiving me, I can hear, at the bottom of the hill, the sound of terror punching the stilled air; they are finally approaching our cluster of secluded roads. I wonder if I am the only target on their list today.

I still can't believe John is hiding in that dirty shed full of broken trap wood and discarded wheels. He has been sleeping in a makeshift tent made of old blankets thrown across splintered wooden posts. Weighted mustiness veiled a second smell; something animalistic which lingered like years of crusted grease. He cannot stay there much longer. Perhaps he will be gone by this evening. When I eventually found the dilapidated structure last night, I followed the instructions about tapping the bottom panel of the door in a particular pattern so that John would recognize me as a friend.

'How on earth did you know where I was, Dervla?' He opened the shed door just enough to let me squeeze inside. His dark cap shadowed his face; I could just about make out the spikey roughness of heavy stubble. Strange, I don't think I've ever seen John with a beard, just his dark moustache. He led me by my arm to a dim corner and we sat beside each other on a cast iron garden bench which was once beautiful. He wore a dark green blanket over his crumpled shirt which itself was partially unbuttoned.

'A message from Seamus was given to me a few hours ago when we were organizing the dinners for Mountjoy. I've been out of my mind with worry about the two of you. I know you both need my help and I think that's why Seamus sent the message. He stayed with us a few weeks ago for the night. He was keeping something from me and I haven't seen him since. My God, John, you look terrible, you need a doctor, have you been wounded, or something?'

He took off his cap and said he was fine, that he'd fallen down some steps near Merrion Square. 'I think I've just bruised a rib, don't worry about me, I just need to lay low for another day or two.' He took two or three mouthfuls of water which I had brought with me. With his dirty hands, he ate less than half a slice of the bread I gave him. It was plain to my eyes how exhausted and agitated he felt. I knew better than to ask him why he was hiding in that disgusting shed.

'Oh John, things have been getting worse over the last few weeks, everyone is terrified to walk in the street, or stay in their house. Those bastards shot an innocent man in Talbot Street. And Mr O'Carroll was murdered in cold blood by soldiers in Manor Street. And another man was gunned down in Mary's Lane.' John stayed quiet for a long moment.

'Dervla, there are other things I need to tell you, I should have told you more before, but it was always better that you and Mam didn't know too much beyond what you did for the movement inside the house. I need you to listen to me now, though,' he said.

My instinct told me not to tell him that someone has been following me, or about the anonymous note.

'We don't have a lot of time John, never mind about the past, I've always known you'd do anything for the cause, just tell me what I can do now.'

'It's complicated, Dervla, I can't put you or the family in any more danger. We feel terrible about that awful night when the military raided the house, it shouldn't have happened, we've always been so bloody careful.' John had tears in his eyes as he spoke.

There was no time to explain that I suspected we were all targets, one way or another.

'John, forget about all that. I heard that the military threw bombs into the tenements on Capel Street the day after Mr O'Carroll was killed. I can't just wait around and do nothing. People everywhere are being terrorized, or waiting to be, when is it going to end?'

Having had so little time with Seamus before, I had promised myself that if I saw John I wouldn't let him see me in a state. I wanted to be strong and useful. At mass I resolved to be brave and invisible. To somehow protect one brother and find the other. And afterwards, at the prison, I received Seamus's message from a lad in his Battalion. But now, John was getting weaker before my eyes. He was beginning to struggle with his breathing. Each breath sounded like it was pushing against a noxious fluid which threatened to flood his fragile airways. I thought of the poisoned gas tearing through so many young lungs in Belgium and France. I thought of Nellie Franny's shallow breath in her last hours. Maybe I could have done something more to save her. I pleaded with John to stop talking and rest for a moment.

'Listen to me, Dervla. Kevin Barry is going to be hanged tomorrow morning for that ambush he was involved in last month. He's refusing to give the names of the others, but if you really want to know what Seamus couldn't tell you–'

'No, don't tell me, John,' I said, putting my fingers to his dry lips. 'It's not important to me, any more. I know now that I should never have stayed in London for so long. My place is here, in Dublin, with my family. You already know I've been working with Cumann na mBan and before that with St Bride's. So please tell me, John, what can *I* do, right now, to help you and the other Volunteers? Surely to God, you must need all the help you can get?'

My older brother took both my hands. They were small, almost childlike, in his own hands. He closed his eyes as if to invite me to pray with him. Or was he asking me for forgiveness? Perhaps we both were. The words of his short letter about Rory framed themselves in my mind. In that small moment, I knew nothing would ever be the same again.

'First of all, before you get any more involved in the movement, I need you to be extremely careful. More so than ever before. All hell could break loose when they execute that young Barry boy. He will be the first since the Rising executions. People will take to the streets, Mountjoy will be mobbed.' When John said this, those horrible words of the other day flooded my

185

thoughts: *Don't expect your brothers or anyone else to be around to protect you from the second raid.* Of course, tomorrow, the raid will be tomorrow, I realized sitting there beside John. After Kevin's hanging. For a moment, this was all I could think about while John was speaking.

'… Michael Collins and the Squad will retaliate. Maybe not immediately, but we will at some point. That means the government will probably plan to carry out more executions. Reprisals will follow reprisals.' John paused and looked at me carefully. He waited for all he'd said to sink in; the deliberate, almost casual link to the Intelligence Squad. The Assassination Unit. Perhaps he didn't know that Seamus had already told me. He let the coarse blanket drop over the back of the bench as he spoke. His thin frame seemed to shrink behind his loosened clothing.

'You need to be ready, Dervla. What I'm saying is that your connection to me and Seamus could, now, more than ever before, make you an immediate target for arrest and harsh interrogation. You must maintain absolute ignorance of anything to do with us; you have not seen or heard from your brothers in months. Do you understand what I'm saying?' He was now addressing the other version of me; he had finally accepted the metamorphosis of one sister into another, more hard-edged, militarized second-sister.

'Yes, I understand, but you have to let me come back with a doctor tomorrow,' I said, 'there's something wrong with your breathing, you need proper medical attention.' I willed myself into a persona of dutiful respect, pragmatic and cool. As I sat on the cast iron bench with John, I knew that this more covert role would, in time, demand absolute detachment and clear objectivity.

'No, you must leave now, don't worry about me, others are helping me. I promise I will send you a message tomorrow with instructions,' he said.

My beloved brother seemed to be dying in front of me in that filthy shed, which served as his sanctuary, and I had to simply abandon him, not knowing if he would survive the night. How could my parting words to him be that already I feared it was too late, that there would probably be a second raid on the house tomorrow, one far more sinister than the first, and that me being arrested for interrogation was the very least of my worries?

***

Still no sign of John's promised message. A thousand things could have prevented him making contact. I cannot wait any longer; it's time to follow my own plan. First, I must finally destroy my treasured diary. My very last entry, hastily scrawled late last night when I finally got home, is chillingly cruel: *Surely we will have a visit from the Black and Tans tomorrow? All will be ready for them to burn the house. What else can I do?*

I am not ashamed of anything I've written in these pages before me. There isn't a word which could not be proudly justified by the love I feel for my little nation. Anyway, it would probably take the military days to decipher my comings and goings, all mixed up with the most ordinary events of daily life. I doubt they would bother trying. The girlish ramblings of someone in the shadow of her I.R.A. brothers. Who cares if she distributed a few handbills for that pathetic propaganda league in London, or if she ran with minor dispatches for that band of women, I can hear them say. But if they did take more than a mildly bemused interest, the entries which would seal my fate for years are not too difficult to find. Some flit and hover in the corners and folds of pages, while others glisten boldly in whole confessional paragraphs.

But I will not give the military any opportunity to smear their oil-grained fingers over my memories, to laugh aloud as they tear apart my private pages which contain the essence, banal and incendiary, of my own life, over the last four years. Nor will they drool over tasty morsels of information which they'd regurgitate on to their own platter of twisted evidence.

I am holding the unlit match in my hand when I hear an urgent banging of a fist against the back door. At the same time, I hear Nuala's voice calling my name. When I unlock the door to let her in, she is wailing, hysterical almost, her hair loosened and dishevelled, a bruised expression locked in her eyes. Her hands are shaking with the cold when I take hold of them and draw her hastily into the scullery.

'The Tans,' she blurts out, 'are sprawled round their armoured cars at the bottom of the hill, smoking and laughing, waiting to make their move on this house, Dervla. Why in God's name are you still here?'

I watch in alarm as my best friend stumbles into the front room and begins to pace erratically beside the fireplace. She gestures with the palms of her hands for me not to approach her, not to say anything. Her words erupt like molten lava from her mouth and seem to engulf the air around us:

It's all my fault, Dervla. What a total fool I've been. If I'd told you what happened maybe we could have prevented the raid back in March. I suppose I had just wanted to impress Niall with a bit of idle gossip about my old friend and her life in the big city. To think he has already spent time in your company since then, those outings we went on after Christmas, remember? I suppose I had been envious of your cultured London life. God, how was I to know how he'd react to it all, ages later? All I did was talk about your perfect Edmund and about Mr Churchfield's horrible letter demanding to know about your background. Even after promising you I'd mention that letter to nobody. Jesus Christ, I thought that was it on the subject, I swear to God.

But he must have latched onto something I'd said because, out of the blue, months later, he wanted to know more about the letter from Edmund's father. You were back home by this stage so it really threw me. He was suddenly very interested to know why an Irish girl in London had brought so much attention upon herself. I told him to forget what I'd said before. That it was just me being irritated by your cosy little world in London, your wonderful English boyfriend, your romantic picnics, your new best friend, Nellie Franny. All this while Dublin was in the hands of the occupying enemy. God, I feel terrible, it was unforgivable to have said such things so flippantly. I mean it's not like I hadn't been aware of your own torments about being in London; how difficult it had been for you to decide to finally come home.

But with Niall hearing what I'd said then made it even worse. Something flipped over in his mind. He glared at me in disgust and became really angry. Him, a loyal Castle government clerk, seen as an *occupying enemy*. He twisted my ordinary words, Dervla. Up to that point he let me think he was a friend·of ours, a total sympathizer, him being Irish and everything. Joining in our discussions about one day being free from all this tyranny. All those lies about his plans to leave the Castle and train to be a printer and to join the boys. He was furious and said he couldn't unhear what I'd said. And what if *you* were a real enemy of the Castle; perhaps that Mr Churchfield suspected something. I was utterly shocked and dumbfounded.

In the end, he told me he had no choice but to make an appointment with a senior clerk in the Under Secretary's office; he said it was his duty to act on what I'd told him. A ridiculous meeting where he remoulded my silly banter into some kind of solid Castle intelligence. He had the audacity to tell the clerk that you may be planning a Westminster sabotage to gain access to strategic information about the workings of the parliament buildings. I could not believe my ears.

Then he tried to cajole me by saying a gentle warning was all it'd be as you were my best friend. The military would probably just ask you a few questions about your time in London; enough to put you off any silly notions, now that you were back in Ireland. I was so confused and upset and I didn't want to admit to anyone that I'd made a monumental mistake by trusting and loving Niall. And I let it happen, Dervla. He knew I wouldn't try to warn you. When I think of your poor mother, and young Mary.

But that's not the worst of it, Dervla. On Thursday night it all came crashing down on top of me. Niall was like a monster, he had been drinking with a crowd from work. He told me he'd been using me the whole time. It was your brothers he and his friends in the Castle were after, all along. My pathetic story about the Churchfields, which they might still have use for, had made it easier for them to distract you so that you'd one day lead them to John and Seamus. That had been their plan, anyway, Niall told me. But judging by the demented mood he was in, it was a plan that didn't work out for them. You are as much of a target to them now.

He took sick pleasure in telling me that a second raid would happen any day now. And that they have new information about that ambush outside Monk's. The drink had him full of talk he was only too delighted to hurl at me. I swear I never, ever mentioned John or Seamus. That would have been unthinkable as they'd been on the run for so long. But Dervla, I've never hidden the fact of our membership with Cumann na mBan. On my life, though, I'm telling you Niall knows nothing of our own few activities. When he manipulated me like that I vowed to keep that part of our lives secret.

But I stayed with him, Dervla, for months and months, good God, what was I thinking? That's why I've been so distant. I tried to pretend none of it actually happened. I screamed at him to tell me when the second raid would be, that they'd be wasting their time because John and Seamus hadn't been seen for a long time. He just laughed in my face and said there would be no-one to witness it. And that when the military were finished destroying your house they might arrest you and throw you in Mountjoy for your Westminster plot. He was so proud of his vicious deceit.

I betrayed you, Dervla, by discussing your private life in London, and by letting my guard down. I was jealous of the life you had, a naive fool in love, so I was. I should have told you then what I'd done, but the shocking way Niall stretched what I'd innocently said into a web of lies and exaggeration paralysed me. I put that note under your door at dawn on Friday, soon after he passed out in my room. I am so sorry and ashamed, Dervla. I knew you wouldn't leave this house, and now the Tans will rampage themselves up here any minute.

***

I stand in complete silence. So, the wiry Poe character *was* sent from the Castle after all, but he has nothing to do with Mr Churchfield. Edmund hasn't divulged incendiary information about my family. His father isn't spying on me, he probably just hates me. His menacing letter last year was no more than personal and pathetic.

I haven't told Nuala about the sporadic contact with Edmund, and she doesn't yet know about his telegram to say he's actually in Dublin, right now. Waiting for me. Still waiting for me. She must have just assumed in her note I was making things worse for myself by being in any kind of contact with him; my Westminster plot. It occurs to me that I probably only ever let Nuala see the brighter side of my life in London, the love-wrapped moments with Edmund. The odd image of her sleeping in her bed, while the military carried out their polite raid, months ago in this house, is an absurd one. Even hearing her tormented confession is too unreal to believe. I wonder does

193

she realize or remember that we'd already received word that the Tans might strike our terrace that week; now I know she was the original source of the attack.

***

My beloved diary looks like a humble offering, a waiting sacrifice, lying flat on top of the fresh sod of turf in the grate. The scratched sound of the striking match grazing firmly against the rough surface on the side of the matchbox is deeply satisfying. Kneeling together, Nuala and I coax and drag the new flame in between the closing, compliant pages. It appears to falter, consider its options for a fraction of a second, before latching on to my memories and spreading its wide, waxy burn in the direction of the patient kindling beneath. In the space of two seconds a single page releases itself from the melting spine and there is just enough time to read the quivering words of an old song, or poem, I now recall I copied from somewhere:

> *Since I have given thee all my very heart,*
> *Since I have staked so deep and dangerously*
> *All that I have of hope till breath depart*
> *And flung my little kingdom on the die.*
>
> *Since now there streams over my land and sea*
> *This dread love - strange as light - beyond recall,*
> *I am thy prisoner; yes, and thou art free*
> *With but a touch to lay in ruin all*

The sweet, welcoming smell of peaty turf, resting on top of tightly twisted newspaper, as bright, young flames rise in the hungry grate, remind me of those who lived and suffered before me. I try to conjure them, our dispossessed, to reach in towards the firelight and beckon them from the bog and ditch grave they call their new home. The bailiff's hatchet and crow bar have tumbled the rest.

I hold Nuala's trembling hand in mine as we raise ourselves from our knees and stand side by side and stare into the fire, in silence. After a long moment, I ask her if she feels the warming presence of our trampled race, our land-starved tribe, our ejected kin. She nods her head without looking at me.

Inside the ferocious beauty of the fire, I can see them clearly now, my own people, their refusal absolute, as their ancient land and defiant souls are kicked by a foreign leather boot, very much like the one now pounding like an angry bull at my front door.

Acknowledgements

My special thanks to May Guilfoyle (1887-1972) whose treasured diaries greatly inspired this book. I also want to thank Michelle Dunne and her family for very kindly lending me May's precious diaries.

As part of my research I read various books including *No Ordinary Women* by Sinead McCoole, *Hanna Sheehy Skeffington Suffragette and Sinn Féiner* by Margaret Ward, *The Republic* by Charles Townsend, *Michael Collins: Dublin 1916-22* by Joseph E. A. Connell Jnr..

Author's note

This work of fiction is inspired by May Guilfoyle's diary entries written from 1917 to 1920. Many of the events and characters in this book do not appear in May's real diary entries. But every now and then she hints that some of the personalities might have been there, bringing joy, forming shadows, as she worked and loved and adventured through her life.

A shorter version of my short story, *Meeting Countess Markievicz*, appears in this book. Here, it forms part of the diary entry, *A Westminster Symbol*.

From 1884 many Dubliners preferred to call their main street O'Connell Street rather than Sackville Street. The name finally became official in 1924.

About the author

Paula Tully was born in Dublin, Ireland. She has an MA in American Literature and a BA in English and History of Art, both from University College Dublin. As well as this novella, *Her Rebel Self*, Paula has also written *Meeting Countess Markievicz and Other Irish Short Stories*, her first collection of short stories.

Connect with Paula Tully

Email: orchidpressdublin@gmail.com
Website: www.paulatully.com
Twitter: @paula_tully
Facebook: facebook.com/paulatullyauthor
Instagram: paula_tully_writer